THE MYSTERIOUS FOUR

HAUNTINGS and HEISTS

DAN POBLOCKI

Scholastic Inc.

**New York   Toronto   London   Auckland
Sydney   Mexico City   New Delhi   Hong Kong**

ISBN 978-0-545-29980-0

12 11 10 9 8 7 6 5 4 3 2 1   11 12 13 14 15 16/0

Printed in the U.S.A.   40
First printing, January 2011

For my grandmother, Wanda Poblocki,
who loves a good mystery

1

THIS ONE STARTS WITH A BANG

The day was hot and the air was still. In her new bedroom, Viola Hart had just unpacked her third box of mystery novels, when a gunshot exploded the afternoon.

Rushing to the window, Viola frantically scanned the street, hoping to catch the culprit in the act. She imagined finding a cop chasing a suspicious-looking woman in a glittering red dress . . . or a couple of mobsters clutching purple velvet bags filled with diamonds as they raced from a burning car . . . or a mad old man trying to chase away the birds from his yard—

Another glass-rattling bang caught Viola's attention. Up the street, a big black car turned the corner, leaving in its wake a gray puff of exhaust. The car's second backfire left her imagination in a similar cloud, and Viola zoomed back to reality.

Just an old car backfiring? *Oh well*, she thought. *There can't be excitement everywhere.*

Or maybe there could be?

Viola kept her eye out for trouble. She spied people coming in and out of some of the houses on her block. The listing branches of huge maple trees reached out over the road. The aroma of a barbecue grill wafted through the screen, tickling Viola's nose, making her mouth water. The sounds of kids playing down the street echoed from the rooftops, stirring something deep inside her.

The street looked as perfectly normal as the one from which she'd moved, but her mother always said, "You never know what's below the surface until you dig."

After she realized that there would be no shoot-out on her new block, she reluctantly returned to her unpacking. Viola's family had arrived at the large white colonial house early that day, and for most of the morning, she had watched the movers unloading furniture, her parents' computers, plants, and endless boxes into the new house. When the movers were done, her mom and dad had asked Viola to begin organizing her bedroom, which she'd been doing ever since.

Reaching for a random box, Viola noticed something shiny on the floor. Looking closer, she realized it was a button. She did not recognize it. Maybe it belonged to whoever had lived here before her. A clue!

She bent down and also found several small snippets of thread. Red. Purple. Yellow. Green. She picked those up, as well as the button. It had a swirling floral shape pressed into it. Most likely the button had come from a woman's garment, so maybe the room had belonged to a woman. The threads told her more. They had been cut short with scissors; each was less than an inch long. She scanned the floor and found more pieces near the closest electric outlet, and she instantly knew what this room had been used for. Viola imagined a sewing machine on a table placed in front of the outlet. The woman had made her own clothes. This had been a sewing room.

Viola placed the button on her bureau. It was worthy evidence. She wondered when she might find more.

She managed to get through most of her clothes and some of her desk supplies before a tickle of sweat trickled down her neck. This time, a cool breeze called to her through the open window. Her best bet for locating clues to her new town was obviously outside. Sixth grade was starting next week, so she had to explore before the summer was over and school began.

"Mom!" Viola called into the hallway. "I got a whole bunch done. Can I go yet?"

"If you have something to say, Viola," her mother replied from downstairs, "please don't shout it for all the neighborhood to hear."

Viola crept past her parents' room, the bathroom, and the empty guest room, then went downstairs and found her mother in the kitchen. She tiptoed across the floor and tapped her mom's shoulder.

Mrs. Hart yelped and spun. "Viola! Don't do that! You scared me."

"Sorry," Viola whispered, even though she was actually proud of her ability to sneak up on people. "I was just trying to be quiet like you asked."

"Well . . . good job, I guess," said her mom, distracted. She had just attached a picture of Viola and the family's golden retriever to the refrigerator with a strawberry-shaped magnet.

"Oh, what a cute pic of Brandy," Viola said wistfully. "Can I put it in my room?"

"Be my guest," said Viola's mother, opening another box atop the counter. "Wow, who packed this one?" She pulled out a small wood plaque— her journalism award. "Does this really belong with the china?" she continued, speaking to herself.

Viola delicately plucked the photo from the

refrigerator. "So, Mom, can I go outside yet? I've got to check out the neighborhood before the sun goes down."

"You still have quite a few hours before that happens."

"Exactly!" exclaimed Viola. "I want to make use of them. There might actually be some mysteries to solve in this town."

Mrs. Hart used to be a crime reporter. In Philadelphia, Viola had loved reading her mother's articles. She had always looked closely at the unsolved crimes, trying to pick out a telling clue that would give away the guilty party—like the time she suggested that a neighborhood gardener was responsible for a string of home robberies. In Viola's opinion, grassy footprints had given him away.

Here in Moon Hollow, Mrs. Hart would be the editor of the local newspaper, the *Moon Hollow Herald*. A huge step up. She glanced from the plaque before placing it on the counter. "I don't want you bothering anyone."

"I won't be a bother," said Viola. "In fact, before this month is over, I'm sure people will be thanking me for all my help."

"Hmm," said Mrs. Hart, with a smirk. "I bet." She paused, then added, "Okay, fifteen more minutes, then you're free for the afternoon."

"Thanks, Mom," answered Viola begrudgingly. She turned and walked back up the stairs, determined to find her detective kit in the boring mess that was her bedroom.

Seventeen minutes later, in the house next to the Harts' new home, the doorbell rang just as Rosie Smithers was sitting down to read. Heaving a sigh, Rosie stood, wondering who it could be. Her older brothers and sisters had all left the house to go to the mall for new school clothes, and Rosie had been looking forward to having some peace and quiet for a change. When you have four older siblings, those times are rare.

Rosie didn't need new clothes. Hers were always hand-me-downs. She knew some of her classmates would have hated wearing old stuff, but Keira and Grace had grown so tall so quickly, the clothes that no longer fit them were usually still in style. Today, she wore her favorite pair of jeans, her worn-out All Star sneakers, and a bright pink tank top. Her grandmother had once told her that pink complemented her light brown skin, so she wore that color often.

Rosie opened the door to find a red-haired girl standing before her.

"Hi," said the girl. "I'm Viola Hart. My family just moved in next door." She nodded toward the house on her right.

Viola was short and a bit plump. She wore an old blue T-shirt with a UPenn logo emblazoned on the front, a pair of khaki shorts with huge cargo pockets, and bright red flip-flops. Her toenails were painted fluorescent green. Her eyes were bright blue and her hair was an explosion of curls. Freckles spattered her nose like flecks of paint. She held a marbled black-and-white composition notebook in her hand.

"Oh, hi," said Rosie. "Nice to meet you. I'm Rosie. I live . . . here." Then, blushing, she added, "Obviously."

"Duly noted," said Viola, pulling a pen from her pocket, opening her notebook, and scribbling on a blank page.

Leaning forward, Rosie tried to get a closer look. "What did you write down?"

"Just that you live here," said Viola. "You never know what you might need to remember." She stared at Rosie for a moment. "Like the fact that you're left-handed."

Rosie was shocked. "How did you know that?"

Viola smiled, then tentatively touched Rosie's right hand, which was covered with doodles of flowers and insects. "I assumed you drew these, and you couldn't have used your right hand to do it. Judging from the quality of the artwork, you must be skilled with your left. So . . ."

Rosie squinted at the new girl. "Right," she answered. "I mean, *correct*. I am left-handed. That was really . . . cool."

"Anyway," Viola continued, "I came over to say hello . . . but also to ask if you know of any mysteries going on in this town."

"Mysteries?" asked Rosie. "What kind of mysteries?"

"Oh, you know . . . anything," said Viola. She glanced quickly over her shoulder, as if she might miss a car chase racing down the street behind her. "Crimes. Murders. Robberies. You know, the usual?"

"I haven't really heard of any lately."

Viola smiled mischievously. "Do you want to try and find some?"

"Robberies? Murders?" said Rosie, her voice getting very small. "Is it safe?"

Viola laughed. "Well, we won't jump into what my mom calls 'the big time' at first. We don't want our parents complaining if we get into trouble. Seriously . . . there are mysteries to solve in all sorts of places, if you know where to look. You just have to pay attention."

Rosie glanced back at the book she had left sitting on the comfy living room chair. *The Secret Lives of Tasmanian Devils*. It could wait. She stepped onto the front porch, closed the door behind her, turned, and smiled. "All right, then," she said. "Let's go pay attention."

Woodrow Knox and Sylvester Cho were hiding underneath Sylvester's back deck, listening to Mr. and Mrs. Cho argue about the proper way to light the grill. The boys had come down below the wooden stairs to add a moat to the secret mini-fortress they'd spent a good portion of their summer designing. Woodrow was focused on security issues, but Sylvester was distracted by something in the distance.

"Who is that with Rosie Smithers?" he asked.

Woodrow looked toward the street where Sylvester was pointing, near the maple tree that separated the Chos' yard from the white colonial. Two girls were standing at the base of the tree, staring up into the branches. Woodrow recognized Rosie immediately—not only was she in his grade at school, but her house was directly behind his own. However, Woodrow didn't know the red-haired girl Rosie was with.

"Hey, do you think her family is the one who moved into the Denholms' old house?"

Sylvester asked. "I saw a truck over there this morning."

"Maybe," said Woodrow. "There's only one way to find out."

The boys left their fort and moat behind, tramping across the grass toward the maple tree. When they reached the two girls, Rosie turned and waved.

"Hi, Sylvester," she said. "Hi, Woodrow."

"Hey," said the boys.

"Woodrow and Sylvester live behind us," Rosie explained to the new girl. Then she turned to the boys. "This is Viola Hart," she said. "She just moved in. She's teaching me about mysteries." Viola, who'd been examining the maple tree's trunk, looked at the boys and scribbled some things in her notebook.

"What kind of mysteries?" asked Sylvester, suddenly curious.

"All kinds," said Viola. "Like you, for instance." Sylvester wore cut-off khakis and a white, short-sleeve, button-down shirt. His black hair was spiked and messy, as if he'd just rolled out of bed—or at least wanted to look like it. "You probably had eggs for breakfast," she said.

Sylvester's mouth dropped open. "How did you know?"

Viola pointed at his chin. "Dried ketchup. I noticed your parents firing up their barbecue grill, which means you haven't had lunch yet. And what do people usually put ketchup on at breakfast? Eggs. I just took a guess. Sometimes it works to just throw something out there and see if it sticks."

Sylvester blushed and rubbed at his chin. "It was a *late* breakfast," he said.

Viola turned to Woodrow, who grew suddenly nervous. His red T-shirt was decorated with a sports team mascot Viola didn't recognize— a bright blue lizard clutching a baseball bat. A large key ring rattled from the belt of his jeans. He had shaggy blond hair and sparkly green eyes.

"You..." She thought for a few seconds. "You probably live in a couple different houses. And you love riding your bike. In fact, I bet you ride your bike more than you ride in cars."

Woodrow nodded his head in wonder. "You're right. I live here with my mom, but my dad lives down in New York City. And yeah, I do love riding my bike. How did you know?"

"You have a whole bunch of keys there," said Viola. "Why would someone our age carry so many keys? You'd need one to get into your own house, and I figured one might be for another house. Or apartment. And I knew that the smaller one was for a bike lock, because it looks just like a key my dad has for *his* bike."

"Okay." Woodrow smiled. "But what are the other keys for?"

"Gimme some time. I'll figure those out too," Viola said with confidence.

"Viola's really good at this," said Rosie, impressed. "She knew I was left-handed because of my doodle-drawings." She showed everyone the pen marks on her right hand.

"Rosie's got talent too," Viola added. "She's the one who pointed out this carving in the tree bark." She scribbled some more notes in her notebook and then flipped the cover shut. "So who do you guys think carved the trunk?" she asked, glancing back at the maple. She pointed with her pen. "See? Right here?"

The boys leaned forward. Sylvester saw a pair of initials sliced into the bark. He'd never noticed them before.

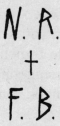

"Huh," said Woodrow. "Weird."

"Do you guys know anyone with those initials?" asked Viola.

The boys shook their heads.

Rosie answered, "From the dark appearance of the wood, I would assume that whoever carved this did it a long time ago."

"Isn't carving your name into a tree supposed to be bad for it?" Woodrow asked. Rosie was good at science and always seemed to know about things like plants and animals and minerals.

"Yeah," she answered, "it cuts off their flow of nutrients. If everyone in this neighborhood did that, the tree would have died a long time ago."

Viola sighed, staring closer at the initials. "But there's something so romantic about it." When no one said anything, Viola looked back to find the boys with their eyebrows raised. "Oh, calm down," she said, poking Sylvester in the arm. "I'm not going to be asking either of you to carve your initials into anything any time soon."

"Ow," said Sylvester, rubbing his bicep. Woodrow snickered.

"Hey," said Viola, "do you guys want to help me and Rosie find a mystery to solve? I have to be home in two hours, but something might catch our eyes before then."

"What, like, in *this* neighborhood?" asked Woodrow.

"Yeah," said Rosie. "Weird stuff is everywhere if you know where to look. I mean . . . that's what I've heard."

Sylvester looked back at his house, where his parents were still arguing about the stupid bar-becue. Woodrow looked farther, toward his own quiet home. His mother was at work.

The boys answered at the same time. "Sure!"

The mystery hunt had begun . . . and they were off!

2

THE FIVE CLUES OF VIOLA HART

The group walked around to the front of the Chos' house and stood on the corner. From there, they had a good view of the rest of the neighborhood.

Although Moon Hollow was nestled into a sheltered valley on the Hudson River, and for the most part looked like an isolated small town, there was still a lot going on.

To their right, down a long wooded embankment, the river flowed like a wet blue marker streak across a green construction-paper canvas. The sun glittered upon the waves, illuminating the air with seasonal magic. Farther downstream, train tracks ran along the riverbank, connecting the town to New York City, which was about an hour south. In the hills above town, the forested campus of Moon Hollow College sat quietly, its clock tower poking up through the trees. Nearby, the Moon Hollow Museum was a

15

destination for city and country people alike, filled with all sorts of art and antiquities. Beyond the nearest ridge, several large hills loomed. Mini-mountains. There was a national park where visitors hiked, picnicked, and sometimes camped.

The kids walked toward Main Street, snaking through alleys, passing a movie theater, grocery stores, restaurants, antique stores, and art galleries. As they investigated, each member of the group told Viola more about him or herself.

Rosie had a large family. Her mother was the town librarian and her father was on the board of the art museum on the hill. Sylvester's parents owned the Main Street Diner, and Sylvester often helped out at the counter after school, doing his homework in between pouring coffee and bussing dishes. Woodrow lived with his mother, who had moved to town several years ago to work at the park in the mountains. His father was a lawyer in New York City. Woodrow tried to visit him as much as possible.

Viola took meticulous notes, jotting down differences between the Hudson Valley and her old town, which had mostly been made up of highways and strip malls and fast-food restaurants.

Eventually, the group made a full circle and stood on the corner in front of Rosie's house.

"We're back," said Rosie, disappointed. "And I didn't notice any mysteries at all."

"What about that house over there?" Viola pointed to the house across the street from her own. It was hidden well behind a thick patch of tall brush, overgrown trees, and spidery, creeping vines.

"Mr. Reynolds's house?" said Rosie. "It's been empty ever since he died last year, but I don't think there's any mystery about it. It's just a creepy old place."

"It's been almost two hours," said Sylvester, turning away from the house across the street. Viola could tell he didn't want to go exploring over there.

She pursed her lips. "Well, maybe we can prolong our search. . . ."

"How?" asked Woodrow. "Don't you have to go home?"

"Exactly," said Viola. "And you guys should come with me. I think my mom made some lemonade for the movers this morning. There should be some left in the fridge."

The group nodded and followed Viola up the sidewalk and past her mom's sedan, which was parked in the driveway.

Once inside, Viola heard her father talking on the phone in his new office next to the living room. Like the rest of the house, the office furniture was a jumble, and the walls were bare. "The first faculty meeting was last week, but I was able to teleconference in. I set up meetings with some of the grad students for tomorrow," he said, glancing at the small group standing in the foyer. He smiled and winked, then turned away and continued his conversation. Upstairs, Mrs. Hart sang to herself as she organized her bedroom.

"Come on," whispered Viola. "Let's go to the kitchen."

Viola managed to find four glasses in one of the boxes and poured everyone some lemonade. They all sat at the cluttered kitchen table, glancing around the room at everything left to be unpacked. Woodrow banged his cup against the table, sloshing liquid onto his hand.

"What's wrong?" Sylvester asked.

"I just had an idea," Woodrow said, reaching for a paper towel, a grin creeping across his face. "We've been looking all over town for a mystery, right? A mystery for Viola to solve."

"With your help," Viola pointed out. She hadn't meant for this afternoon to be all about her. "You know, like a game?"

"A mystery game," said Woodrow. "We've been *looking* for a mystery to solve all afternoon, while Viola's been solving mysteries the whole time,"

"She has?" said Sylvester.

"Yeah," Woodrow said. "She's solved the mysteries of *us*. Well, we've had our own mystery to solve too. We just didn't realize it."

"What is it?" asked Rosie, sitting up straight. "What's the mystery?"

"Viola," answered Woodrow.

"Viola?" Sylvester looked confused. "What did she do?"

"She didn't *do* anything," said Woodrow. "But we don't know anything about her."

"Huh," said Rosie, looking at Viola quizzically.

"Yeah," said Sylvester, "we've told you all about ourselves, but you haven't clued us in about yourself, Viola."

Viola turned cherry-bomb red. "I'm sorry! I was just so concerned with taking notes and finding—"

"Don't apologize," said Woodrow. "If you'd told us about yourself, we wouldn't have a mystery to solve right now."

"She's not much of a mystery if she's sitting right here," said Sylvester. "All we have to do is ask her about herself."

"Here's where the game comes in," said Woodrow.

"Right!" said Rosie, turning quickly to Viola. She reached out and pretended to zip Viola's lips shut. "From now until we solve the mystery of Viola Hart, you're not allowed to tell us anything about yourself."

"We'll use clues we find around your house to figure out who you are," said Woodrow. "When we're done, we'll present you with a list of our conclusions. You'll tell us if we were right or not."

"That sounds like fun," said Viola, secretly thankful that she hadn't yet unpacked her under-wear. "Here—you can borrow my notebook if you want."

"Perfect," said Rosie, gulping down the rest of her lemonade. "Are you guys ready to get started?"

"Sure," said Sylvester.

Woodrow picked up Viola's notebook and pen. The group began to tour the house, and Viola stayed not far behind, watching inquisitively. The three wandered through almost every room, keeping their voices low. Woodrow took notes.

Upstairs, Viola introduced everyone to her mother, who seemed happy that Viola had made friends so quickly. The group snooped around Viola's messy bedroom and around the guest room down the hallway. When they peeked into the bathroom, Viola momentarily wondered if this had been a bad idea. There was something embarrassing about looking at toilets with other people. To her relief, the group didn't stay in that room very long.

Downstairs, her father finally hung up the phone and greeted the group. Viola was quick to ask him not to tell her friends anything about himself just yet, explaining that they were in the midst of a mystery game. Mr. Hart seemed confused but let them go about their business.

Finally, Rosie, Sylvester, and Woodrow huddled together. After a few moments, they requested that Viola leave the room. She happily obliged. Viola sat on the front steps outside and stared at her new neighborhood. Behind her, inside, she heard her new friends whispering.

What would they say? Would they be right on, or would their guesses be totally wrong? Would they joke that her middle name was Kiki or Brunhilda or Puddles? What if they found her life to be really, truly boring? Sure, Rosie, Sylvester, and Woodrow all seemed nice enough. But that hadn't stopped people from being mean before. *Maybe*, thought Viola, *I should have started off here differently*. Now there was a mystery for you: how to act on the first day in a new town.

The door opened behind her and the porch creaked with footfalls.

"We've got you pegged, Viola," Woodrow teased.

"Cool," Viola said, trying to sound like her usual confident self. "Bring it on."

"Why don't we head into the backyard," Sylvester suggested. "My parents are probably wondering where I am, and that way they can see me."

"Mine too," said Rosie. "We can sit where our yards meet." The kids headed around the side of Viola's house.

"Yeah," said Woodrow. "We've got all four corners now that you've moved in, Viola."

Viola laughed. "If we wanted, we could stand in all of our yards at once."

"Whoa . . . you're right," said Sylvester. "I get to try it first!" When they reached the place where their yards seemed to come together, Sylvester jumped into the middle of it. The spot was merely a patch of grass, not unlike the rest of the lawn that surrounded them—green, soft, and a bit damp. "Hmm," said Sylvester. "I thought this would be more exciting."

"Speaking of excitement," said Rosie, "let's share our investigation with Viola."

"Yeah," said Woodrow, "let's see if we were right." All four kids sat down in their respective yards, leaning toward one another in anticipation. Woodrow opened Viola's notebook. "So we're going to tell you some stuff we came up with. You have to tell us if we're right. But then your part is to guess how we knew."

"Okay," said Viola. "Cool."

"Our first guess," said Woodrow. "You moved here from Pennsylvania."

Viola's face burned with surprise. "Hey! You're right!"

"How did we know?" asked Woodrow.

Viola glanced back at her new house. In her mind's eye, she removed the outer wall, trying to imagine each room as if the building were a giant dollhouse filled with all her secrets. After a moment, she realized that the answer wasn't inside the house, but next to it, in the driveway. Not more than an hour earlier, the group had strolled by their first clue.

"The license plate on my mom's car," said Viola with certainty. "The state is printed there. That's how you knew I'm from Pennsylvania." She looked down at her T-shirt. "My UPenn shirt probably clued you in too."

"Right!" said Woodrow, passing the notebook to Sylvester. "Nice job."

"You're good at this, Viola," said Sylvester.

"Well, that one was pretty easy," Viola replied.

"Okay, next guess," Sylvester continued. "Your mom is a writer."

"Yup, again. She's actually going to be an editor now, at the local paper. You guys are really good at this too."

The other three gave high fives across their small circle.

Viola thought back on the events of the day. So much stuff was still packed up in boxes, but maybe there had been something lying around that gave away her mother's job.

"So, how did we know?" asked Sylvester.

Earlier that afternoon, just before Viola had asked if she could go outside, her mother had unpacked something from the box on the kitchen table. Viola was certain this object had provided the clue. "Was it my mother's journalism award?" she asked.

"Yes, it was," said Sylvester. "I noticed it sitting on the counter when we first came in for lemonade."

"My turn?" Rosie asked, holding out her hands for the notebook. "You ready for another, Viola?"

"I think so."

"Okay. Our next guess about you is . . . you used to have a dog."

Viola wasn't expecting this one. She closed her eyes, then, trying not to get weepy, she slowly nodded. The rest of the group was quiet, unsure how to respond. Finally, Viola pulled herself together and answered, "Brandy got sick last year. She didn't make it."

Rosie reached out and grabbed Viola's hand. "I'm sorry."

"It's okay," said Viola. "I'm glad you guys noticed. I know exactly what clued you in."

"What was it?" Rosie asked.

"The picture of me and Brandy that I brought up to my bedroom," Viola continued. "I want to get it framed."

"That's right," said Rosie. "I noticed the picture, but didn't see Brandy anywhere. We figured she might be sleeping, but then we noticed there weren't any dog toys or food bowls around either."

"Very perceptive," said Viola. "You guys are learning all about me."

"Ready for another?" Woodrow asked, reaching for the notebook. He seemed eager to change the subject. Viola nodded. "Okay, here were go. You don't have any brothers or sisters."

Viola perked up. "And I'm happy to keep it that way!" She giggled to herself.

"Oh, I know what you mean," said Rosie. "With all my brothers and sisters, sometimes I wish I was an only child too."

"Totally," Sylvester chimed in. "My baby sister can be so annoying sometimes."

"Well, I'm an only child too," said Woodrow. "But sometimes I wish I had a brother to just be brothers with."

"But you got me, dude," said Sylvester, nudging Woodrow with his sneaker toe.

"You're not my brother," said Woodrow. "You're just my best friend."

"Stop, please!" cried Sylvester. "You're gonna make me all emotional."

Everyone laughed.

Finally, Woodrow asked, *"So, Viola, how did we know?"*

"Hmm," said Viola. "Besides the fact that you saw only me and my parents inside my house?" The other kids nodded. "I know! The empty bedroom in the hallway upstairs." Woodrow smiled. She was right. "If I had any siblings, that room wouldn't have been empty."

"Okay," said Sylvester, as Woodrow handed the notebook to him, "last guess."

"I'm ready," said Viola.

Sylvester cleared his throat dramatically. Standing, he read as if making a speech, "We, the members of the Four Corners Mystery Club, believe that Viola Hart's father is a professor at Moon Hollow College."

Viola threw herself back into the soft grass and snorted with laughter. "The Four Corners Mystery Club?" she managed to say. "Who came up with that?"

"I did," said Sylvester. "Just now. You guys want to be part of it?"

"Yeah!" they all answered.

"But, Viola," Rosie added, "you didn't answer the question. Were we right?"

"You sure were."

"So how'd we guess?" asked Sylvester, sitting again.

29

"Let's see," said Viola, racking her brain. Might they have seen her father's diploma in his office? No. First, she didn't think he had actually unpacked it yet. Besides, a diploma wouldn't say that her father was a professor. Could they have read about his appointment in the newspaper? Uh-uh, Viola considered. None of her new friends seemed like the type to be interested in reading those kinds of articles, if there had even been an article to read in the first place. The clue had to have been something that the kids had encountered inside the house. Had her father said anything to them about himself after he'd hung up from his phone call?

No, Viola thought, but he *had* said something before, just as they'd all come in the front door.

"You overheard my dad say that he'd missed the first faculty meeting last week and had to call in for the teleconference," said Viola. "He admitted being a member of a faculty. And he also mentioned his grad students, which meant it had to be college. And since there's only one college around here . . ."

"You are a rock star!" said Sylvester.

"Hardly," said Viola, taking back her notebook. "But thanks."

"We should do this again soon," said Woodrow.

"Oh, can we, please?" said Rosie.

"School starts in a few days," said Viola, "but that shouldn't stop us from meeting right here, where the four corners come together, whenever we feel like it. Mysteries are everywhere, if we look for them."

After their parents began to call the kids home, the group said good-bye. Viola's heart thumped as she came around the front of her new house. Smiling, she climbed the porch steps.

Mysteries are *everywhere*, she thought. And now she had three friends to help her find them.

3

EVEN DETECTIVES GET GOOSE BUMPS

The first night in the new house, Viola awoke to a tapping sound. She sat up and listened, and the noise stopped. Viola wondered if she'd dreamt it, but then it started up again. For a moment, she worried that someone was at her bedroom window. But that was impossible—she was on the second floor.

Viola crept out of bed and into the hallway.

Her parents' door was closed. If they'd heard anything, they didn't seem to mind. Viola tiptoed to the top of the staircase, sharpening her ears to pick up any hint of sound. And there it was. Downstairs. A tiny, repetitious tapping, soft and dull, like a spoon on wood.

In her old house, sometimes the pipes popped and snapped when the heat turned on. Once, a mouse got in under the kitchen sink and made a *scritch-scratch*ing noise at night as it bit through a box of doggie treats. This sound was not like either of those. It was creepier, as if someone were downstairs searching for something—a way in, perhaps. Viola steeled herself, then slowly descended to the small foyer. The tapping wasn't coming from beyond the front door.

Instinct brought Viola to the door that led to the basement. She turned the knob and pulled the handle. The darkness down there was darker than the darkness up here, and Viola couldn't stop chills from racing across her skin. Especially when the sound echoed up the stairs.

"H-hello?" she said, her voice weaker than she wished. And it stopped. Viola closed her eyes as she reached around the doorjamb, searching for a light switch. She found it and flicked it, but nothing happened. Either the bulb was a dud, or the socket was empty. Viola listened to her own breath passing back and forth through her lips. After several minutes, she decided that whoever (or whatever) had been down there was either hiding or gone.

As she crept back upstairs and into bed, thinking about terrible possibilities, Viola's love of mysteries dampened with fear. She stared at the wavering shadows of leafy branches on the ceiling and then remembered the best remedy for this weird feeling. Daylight.

The next morning was busy, and, even if she'd had the nerve, Viola barely had time to think about exploring the basement. Her mother insisted on taking her along to run errands while Mr. Hart met his students at the college. They stopped at the grocery store and hardware store and finished at the pharmacy, where Mrs. Hart let Viola pick out a pack of pencils with fluorescent green erasers—Viola's favorite color.

By the time they pulled into the driveway, Viola was practically bouncing off the ceiling. "Can I go find my friends?" she asked, whipping open the door, one foot already on the asphalt.

"After you help unload the car," said her mom.

Viola pressed her lips together to stop from groaning.

Later, Viola visited each of the three houses that bordered her backyard, but no one was home. After running back to her house and grabbing paper, a pen, and a roll of tape, she stuck notes to her neighbors' front doors.

Who: The Four Corners Mystery Club
(You know who you are.)
What: Official Meeting
Where: The Four Corners (of course!)
When: Today (ASAP)

By late afternoon, Woodrow and Rosie had found their way to the backyard and met Viola, who was sitting in the grass with her notebook.

"Thanks for coming," said Viola when Sylvester, who'd been at his parents' restaurant all day, finally showed up. "I think I need your help." She told them about the noises she'd heard coming from the basement the previous night.

Rosie gasped.

"What's the matter?" said Viola.

"My mom was friends with the couple who lived there before you moved in. Mrs. Denholm used to complain that she heard noises at night too. She wondered if the house was haunted."

"Haunted?" said Sylvester. "Like . . . by a ghost?"

"No," Woodrow said, rolling his eyes, "by leprechauns."

"Really?" Sylvester blushed, glancing around the yard, as if he might catch a glimpse of one. "Here? In Moon Hollow?"

"You want us to check it out with you?" Woodrow asked, ignoring his friend.

"Well, I suppose so," said Viola, happy that she didn't have to suggest it herself.

Less than a minute later, the group stood at the top of the Harts' staircase. Even with afternoon light pouring in the back of the house, the basement was pitch-black. Viola thought that she wouldn't be as terrified surrounded by her new friends, but staring into the shadows, she couldn't stop her imagination from running wild—especially after what Rosie said about the ghost. Viola tried the light switch again, but it still didn't work.

"Maybe a flashlight would help," said Rosie.

Upstairs, Viola removed a small box from under her bed—her detective kit. She opened the box and found her old plastic flashlight. She flicked it on, and it emitted a dim glow.

"The batteries are low, but I guess this will have to do," she said, meeting the group back at the basement door. Viola took a deep breath as she led the way down, the others following closely behind her.

Downstairs, they found an empty room with a low ceiling. A cracked, concrete floor spread out before them, leading to a small hole in the corner—a sub-pump, Viola recognized from her old house, in case of flooding. A row of wooden shelves lined one wall, but other than that, there didn't even seem to be a place where someone might make the tapping sound Viola had heard the night before. The walls were old stone.

"Huh," said Sylvester. "There's nothing here.

No way to get in or out except for the stairs, and you said you were standing there last night."

"Maybe someone was down here, but they waited for you to leave before they crept back up and snuck out of the house," said Rosie.

Viola grimaced. "Somehow, I think I'd be more comfortable with a ghost."

"I guess all you can do is wait and listen to see if you hear it again," said Woodrow. "Looks like we've got another mystery to solve, though this one might be a little more difficult than the first one."

"It might take some time," said Rosie. "But I'm sure there's a rational explanation," she added uncertainly.

"Speaking of mysteries," said Viola, relieved to lead the way back upstairs, "I have an idea. Let's go back outside."

4

THE QUESTION OF THE MAKESHIFT COMPASS

They sat on the lawn in the Four Corners. The sun was headed toward the line of trees at the horizon. "So," said Viola, cradling her ever-present notebook, "if we're really going to do this whole mystery club thing, we should make it official."

"How?" said Rosie.

"I have a few ideas," said Viola, opening her notebook. "First, I think we should make a plan to meet here when we can."

"That's easy enough," said Woodrow. "Your notes on our doors worked."

Viola nodded. "I was thinking we should each bring a mystery to the meeting."

"How do you 'bring a mystery' to a meeting?" asked Sylvester.

"By telling a story?" Rosie offered.

"Exactly," said Viola. "We pay attention to

weird stuff we notice around town. Like, say we read about a crime in the newspaper. We try to figure out the clues that lead to the culprit. Then, here, we can challenge each other to figure out the solution. We might even be able to help people out . . . without, you know, being too nosy."

"Oh, Sylvester loves being nosy," said Woodrow. "So that might be a problem for him."

"*You're* nosy!" Sylvester shot back.

"You're nosier!"

"You're the nosiest!" Sylvester leapt across the small circle and tackled Woodrow. They rolled on the grass trying to grab at each other's noses, laughing hysterically.

The girls just looked at each other and shook their heads. "Anyway," said Viola, "what do you think?"

"I think we can do it," said Rosie. "It'll be nice to have something to do that doesn't belong to my brothers and sisters first."

"Yeah," said Viola. "This will belong just to us." She opened up her notebook. "I was looking at the notes you guys took yesterday when you tried to solve the mystery of *me*." Out of breath, the boys finally settled down and paid attention. "There were five questions you guys came up with." She stared at the notebook and bit her lip.

"Maybe for each story we bring to the group, we can categorize the mystery by the number of questions."

Woodrow paused, thinking. "Every mystery has a certain number of questions behind it, right? Like, every question led us to another answer about Viola."

"I like that," said Viola. "Questions." She wrote this in her notebook, clicking open her pen over and over. "Our first case, *The Five Clues of Viola Hart*, was a Five-Question-Mark Mystery. I think judging on the difficulty of every story we bring to the meeting, we can assign a number of question marks to each mystery. We can have One-Mark Mysteries or two or three. Every number gets harder and harder. Although we should probably have a limit. Let's say six."

"So a Six-Mark Mystery would be the hardest to solve?" Sylvester asked.

"Yeah," said Viola. "What do you guys think?" Everyone nodded. "All right, then. So . . . what else?"

"What else what?" said Woodrow.

"For the mystery club," said Viola.

"The Question Marks," said Sylvester. "Do you guys like that name better than the Four Corners?"

Everyone nodded in agreement.

Rosie raised her hand. "What if each of us had nicknames?"

"Yeah!" said Sylvester. "I'll be *Sly Fox, Master of Illusion.*"

Woodrow cracked up. "Master of Idiocy is more like it."

"Watch it, dude," Sylvester said, warning him with a wave of nose-tweaking fingers.

"Um," Rosie continued, "I was thinking of something a little more . . . simple."

"Like what?" said Viola.

"Well," said Rosie, leaning forward, "we've got four corners. Four yards. Four quadrants where each of us belongs. What if our nicknames corresponded to our quadrant? Like on a map?"

"How?" Woodrow asked. ***"What kind of four-way nickname would come from a map?"***

"North, South, East, and West?" said Viola.

Rosie beamed. "Right! A compass. Your house is in one quadrant—you get the corresponding nickname. Like if my house sits in the north, call me North . . . at least here at these meetings."

"Hmm," said Sylvester. "People would think we were weird if I saw you in math class, and I was like, 'Hey, what's up, North?' And you were like, 'Uh, Canada.'"

"That's why you wouldn't *say that* to me in math class," Rosie said, raising an eyebrow.

"No, I like it," said Woodrow. "It's cool, like we're in a spy video game or something."

"I like it too," said Viola. "Do any of you have a compass so we can figure out whose house sits where?" Everyone shook their head. "Shoot. I think I have one that I got at a science museum packed away somewhere, but I have no idea what box it's in. I should have put it in my detective kit."

"We don't need a compass," said Woodrow. "We can make one. I read about it in a book. All we need is a magnet, a cup of water, a cork, and a sewing needle."

"Dude," said Sylvester, "if none of us even has a compass, how the heck do you expect us to find all that other stuff?"

"I'm positive I can find a cup of water at home," said Woodrow, crossing his arms.

Rosie spoke up. "We actually don't need that stuff. All we need is right here with us."

"What do we have?" said Viola, looking around the yard. All she saw was grass, the maple tree with the initials carved into it, and their four houses.

"We have another mystery," Rosie said, leaning back, proud of herself. *"How do we find our way without a compass?"*

"The sun!" Woodrow shouted, pointing toward the trees where the sun was descending. "It always sets in the west."

"And that's all we need to figure out the rest of the compass," said Viola.

"Hey!" said Sylvester. "So I guess I'm West."

"And I'm South," said Woodrow.

"East," said Rosie.

"And North," said Viola, pointing at herself. "Cool. Nice job, Woodrow."

Rosie smiled. "Good job, everybody. We just solved our first Two-Mark Mystery!"

Viola was nervous to climb into bed that night. What if the tapping sounds returned? What if they were closer this time, not just in the basement? During dinner, she'd mentioned it to her parents, but they didn't seem concerned. "Old houses make strange noises," they told her. After hearing that, she decided to keep Rosie's ghost story a secret.

In her room, she distracted herself with thoughts about the mystery club. If things in her house got weirder, she was happy to have help.

When morning came, Viola realized she'd fallen asleep without distraction.

The next few days rushed by. One afternoon,

Woodrow invited Viola, Sylvester, and Rosie to go swimming up at Loon Lake in the mountains. Mrs. Knox drove. They splashed and raced and cannonballed off the small floating platform out in the middle of the water. The whole day passed, and no one could think of any mysteries. Viola wondered if the club might have already solved its last.

Then, the evening before school started, Sylvester frantically knocked on each of their front doors, calling the group to the backyard. Viola asked her parents' permission, then, grabbing her notebook, rushed to find her friends at the Four Corners.

When they were all seated, Sylvester began his story.

5

THE CASE OF THE PSYCHIC SWINDLE (A ?? MYSTERY)

"Everyone already knows I help my parents out at the diner sometimes, even more now that my mom is home a lot with my baby sister, Gwen. We have our regular customers, but we also get a whole bunch of people passing through. Sometimes, the *passers* are really weird."

"Weirder than you?" Woodrow teased.

Sylvester rolled his eyes and continued. "Today, breakfast was freakishly busy. I was bussing tables, filling water glasses, stuff like that, when I saw a group of regulars crowded around a booth near the front window. My dad was in the back, talking with one of the cooks, so I went over to see what was going on.

"Sitting in the booth were an old woman and a little boy. She looked my grandmother's age, and he was maybe six or seven, I guess. She wore this long multicolored tunic thing that draped down to the floor. Around her neck were bunches of shimmery glass beads. She had on these huge bifocal glasses that made her appear bug-eyed. The kid was pretty normal, I guess, except that he sort of looked embarrassed to be there sitting across the table from her. If they were from Moon Hollow, and I don't think they were, they'd never come into the diner before.

"She was shuffling a deck of cards, and the crowd was getting bigger and bigger. She'd told everyone that her grandson, Louie, could read her mind. The regulars laughed at first but realized she was serious. Even though they didn't really believe her, everyone was curious to see what she was talking about."

"Me too," said Rosie, leaning forward.

"I love card tricks," Sylvester went on. "Woodrow can tell you that I'm always on the lookout for a new one, so I was probably the most curious of all. But the woman made her eyes even wider and promised that this was no trick. She insisted that Louie was a genuine *psychic*.

"She handed the cards to Mr. Lawrence, this big truck driver dude who stops for breakfast every morning. She told him to shuffle. Mr. Lawrence mixed up the cards really well, straightened them out, then handed them back to her. She put the deck facedown on the table in front of her. I watched her the entire time just to make sure she didn't try anything funny. Louie looked scared, but she smiled at him and grabbed his hand and didn't let go, then she took a card from the top of the deck. She kept the card hidden from him, held it in front of her face, then squeezed her eyes shut in concentration.

"Then, really quietly, Louie guessed. 'Is it the jack of spades, Gramma?'

"The old woman opened her eyes and smiled, showing us the card. Everyone gasped. It *was* the jack of spades.

"Mr. Lawrence grabbed the card from her, examining it closely, and asked her how the heck she'd done it. She only smiled wider, looking like she'd just gotten away with something. 'We're psychic,' she said. 'I already told you that.' Then she added, 'We can do it again. Maybe you'd like to make a wager that we can't.'

"Mr. Lawrence turned red and said, 'You got a bet, lady.' And he pulled out a twenty. 'But this time, I get to pick the card.'

"'Suit yourself,' she said. 'But I still need to hold it, so I can concentrate on sending my psychic waves to Louie here.'

"Mr. Lawrence glanced at Louie. 'How about you let go of the kid's hand?' he said to the old woman. 'You might be giving him some sort of message with a squeeze or a tap or something.'

"With a flabbergasted sigh, the woman released Louie's hand. 'Is everybody ready now?' she asked."

"Weren't you scared that there would be trouble?" asked Viola.

"Yeah, I was pretty nervous," said Sylvester. "At that point, I started looking around for my dad, but it was all happening so quickly, I couldn't find him in time. Mr. Lawrence shuffled the cards, then pulled one from the middle of the deck and handed it to the woman. Again she held it up in front of her face, so that Louie was looking at the back of the card. This time he guessed it was the ace of hearts. Right again."

"So *weird*," said Woodrow.

"The crowd went wild. People were insisting that it was just another lucky guess. This made the old woman smile even more. She asked them all to place their bets that he couldn't do it a third time. But by then, I knew her game.

"Everyone who comes to the diner regularly knows who I am. That's why it wasn't hard for me to speak up and tell them all that they'd better not place any more bets. They were destined to lose."

"Because Louie *was* psychic?" asked Woodrow.

"Absolutely not," said Sylvester. "It was a trick after all. *How did it work?*"

"Her big bifocal glasses were acting like mirrors. Every time she held a card in front of her face, Louie caught a glimpse of it reflected in the glass. That's how he knew what each card was. He wasn't psychic at all. And neither was she.

"Well, I knew that if I called her out on it, the regulars would totally freak out. Mr. Lawrence can be pretty scary sometimes. He'd already given the woman twenty bucks. I had to get her and Louie out of the diner quickly—and the best way to do that was to show her that I knew what she was up to. But I had to do it without telling the crowd that they had been fooled. *Do you know how I got the old woman out of the diner without making a scene?"*

"I stepped forward and told her to try the trick again without wearing her glasses. She threw me the dirtiest look ever, but I stared her down. She knew she'd been caught. She mumbled something about being late for a meeting. I told her I'd get her bill so she could pay, and this made her even angrier. Scrambling to get up, she left the twenty Mr. Lawrence had bet her on the table. 'Keep the change,' she told me. She and Louie were out the door before any of the regulars even knew what had just happened."

"Ha!" Viola laughed.

"I took the money off the table and tried to hand it back to Mr. Lawrence. He didn't want to take it, saying she had won it from him fair and square and that my father needed it to pay for the food she ate. I knew there was nothing fair about what she'd done, but instead of arguing, I said okay. Then I slipped the twenty into his pocket when he turned away from me. Just like magic."

6

THE SUPER-SPEEDY TEAM'S TRICK
(A ?? MYSTERY)

Thrilled by Sylvester's excellent powers of obser-
vation and persuasion, the group said good night,
more determined than ever to pay attention to
mysterious events around them.

The first day of school came and went with
little fanfare. Rosie was thrilled to learn that her
science class would be dissecting earthworms
before the end of the year. Sylvester was disappointed that, yet again, he was forced to sit at the
front of each of his classes. Woodrow was curious
and slightly frightened that some of the girls
seemed to be staring at him in the hallways. And
Viola tried to be as outgoing as possible without
seeming like a weirdo—or a zombie. The night
before, she'd briefly thought she'd heard the tapping sounds again. Even though they did not
return before morning, she had not slept well.

The four of them all shared a few of the same classes, during which they passed along the message to meet once more in their yards after finishing any homework or chores.

As the sun was setting, they found one another in the usual spot.

"North, South, East, and West," said Sylvester. "All present and accounted for."

This time, it was Woodrow's turn to tell a story.

"This one is more of a puzzle than a mystery, but I still think it fits our game.

"In my gym class this morning, Coach Winslow divided us all up into teams of six and gave each team a Ping-Pong ball. He told us that whichever team could pass the ball to every member of the group fastest would win the contest. We were allowed to toss the ball to each other any way we chose—rolling, bouncing, flicking. . . . The only rules were that everyone had to touch the ball at least once, and the ball had to move— we couldn't just hold it in place.

"It seemed simple enough to me. I convinced my team that if we stood in a tight circle with our hands really close, our time would be the fastest.

"When Coach Winslow came over to us with his stopwatch, our time was ten seconds, the fastest in the class. We'd won, I figured, which was awesome, because you all know I love to win. But then Coach Winslow shook his head. He told us that last year, a team accomplished the exercise in less than a second.

"We all went back to the drawing board, trying to figure out how that speed was possible. No matter how many times we passed the ball around our circle, we couldn't get it through each of our hands in less than a second. Then, I had an idea that I knew couldn't fail. *What was it?*"

"Since we were all standing so close together, I suggested that we stack our right hands on top of each other, curling our fingers to form a wide tube, as if we were gripping an invisible baseball bat." The group looked at him with interest. *"So what did we do next?"*

"All I had to do to get the ball to pass through all our hands was drop it into the top of the tube. The ball fell to the floor in less than a second.

"And the best part was: We won!"

7

THE PILFERED POOCH
(A ??? MYSTERY)

"That was great, Woodrow," said Viola. "I've got one too. This happened last night after dinner, and I've been saving it up all day just to tell you guys.

"My mom started work at the *Herald* a couple days ago, but she's already off and running with assignments. One of the pieces she was editing had to do with a missing dog. She knows how much I love trying to figure this stuff out. I used to do it all the time when she wrote for the Crime Beat section of the Philadelphia paper. It's how I fell in love with mysteries in the first place. Anyway, my mom let me read the new article. This is the gist of it.

"A husband and wife came home from the movies one night to find their Lhasa apso, Foofy, had been stolen. On their kitchen table, someone had left a note. The letters had been cut out of a magazine."

"That's so disturbing," whispered Rosie.

Viola opened her notebook and pulled out a photocopied page. The mishmash of letters formed the note. She passed it to the group, and they read through it carefully.

WE'VE SEEN YOU WALKING YOUR DOG, FOOFY, AND WE FELL IN LOVE WITH HER. HER FLUFFY HAIR IS ESPECIALLY EXTRORDINARY. WE COULDN'T RESIST TAKING HER. PLEASE DO NOT BE FRIGHTENED. DO NOT LOOK FOR HER. WE WILL GIVE her A GOOD hOME.

"Obviously, the husband and wife were upset. They called the police. The cops came to their home, but found no evidence of forced entry. In fact, the dognappers were thoughtful enough to steal all the dog food, Foofy's water bowl, her leash, and her doggie bed. The couple said that they hadn't noticed anyone strange hanging around the house, but that Foofy did get plenty of attention at the groomer's on Main Street and whenever they brought her to the vet. The police said they would try to track Foofy down, but they really didn't have much to go on.

"Devastated, the wife contacted the newspaper, asking if they would print her husband's written response, pleading for help from the community and possibly even the dognappers themselves. This is the husband's statement." Viola pulled another folded photocopy from her notebook to show the group. This one was handwritten.

PLEASE RETURN FOOFY SAFELY TO HER TRUE HOME. SHE FRIGHTENS EASILY AND LOVES MY WIFE ESPECIALLY. OUR DOG IS QUITE EXTRORDINARY, AND WE MISS HER. WE WILL EVEN GIVE A SUBSTANTIAL REWARD IF SOMEONE HELPS FIND HER.

"I told my mom I'd have to give it some thought. When I woke up this morning, I read the finished article in the paper. I was instantly certain who had written the ransom note. **Who was it?**"

"It was the husband! I told my mother that he was the dognapper and that she should contact the police immediately. Of course, she raised her eyebrows at me, insisting that I couldn't just go around accusing victims of committing their own crimes. My mom asked me, *'How can you be so sure?'*"

"The ransom note and the husband's statement both misspelled the same word. *Do you know which word?"*

"In both letters, the word 'extraordinary' was spelled incorrectly. The first 'a' was missing. I only noticed the difference when I compared the handwritten photocopy of the statement to the corrected version of it in the newspaper. The handwritten misspelling leapt out at me. The same person had written both letters. I knew the husband wrote the second letter, so he must have written the first one too.

"When I got home from school today, my mom called me from her office and gave me the scoop. She said she'd contacted the police. They questioned the husband, confronting him with the proof I'd discovered in the ransom note. And he confessed! He said that Foofy had chewed up his slippers one time too many. He'd secretly arranged for the dog to live with another family several towns away. He couldn't bring himself to tell his wife what he'd done, so he pretended the dog was dognapped."

"Wow, Viola," said Rosie, stunned. "That was a full-on, capital-*D* Detective move!"

"But what's going to happen to Foofy?" asked Woodrow.

"I'm not sure," said Viola. "But I think she's probably going to stay with her new family, at least until the husband and wife can work out their differences."

Rosie leaned forward, looking nervous. "Does the husband know who told on him? What if he's mad at you, Viola?"

"He wouldn't try anything," Viola said. "Besides, the police wouldn't have told him anything about me or my mom helping them out."

At least, she hoped not. . . .

The sun had set. Evening shadows had silently crept across the neighborhood. Frogs still chirped in the trees, but the air had a new chill.

Bang!

Something exploded nearby, and the entire group leapt from the ground. The sound of an old engine raced up the street. Viola remembered her first afternoon in the new house, when she'd heard the noise before. "Just a bad muffler," she explained. "Whoever that old car belongs to really needs to get it fixed."

"You can say that again," answered Woodrow, as they inched away, north, south, east, and west, toward the comfort of their houses. "Good night!"

8

SMALL TOWN SECRETS

Later, Woodrow sat in bed. He'd laid his paused portable video-game player on the mattress and pushed back the curtain from his bedroom window. The lights were on in his friends' houses, and he glanced at the spot on the lawn where the mystery club met. The sky above the town was glowing with great clusters of constellations. Up here, north of the city, the stars were a marvel to behold. It was amazing how many of them hid behind the light pollution down in New York.

Tonight's gathering had been a little embarrassing. The story he had brought was nowhere near as exciting as Viola's. She'd managed to solve a crime—or a sort-of crime. At the very least, she'd solved a real, true mystery.

He listened to the sounds of the local news coming from the downstairs television. His mom had come home late from work again. He hadn't spoken to his dad in a couple days. Maybe if he went down to visit him soon, they'd have a dangerous encounter that Woodrow could bring back and share with the group. Usually, though, his dad would just make frozen pizza and they'd go to an action movie. Boring stuff.

Just then, a great blue streak broke away from a cluster of stars and raced across the darkness. A shooting star! A few seconds later, he watched another one fall. Then another. So cool. This must be a meteor shower. More importantly, Woodrow knew it was a sign. He decided that he needed to do *something* to impress everyone.

In Sylvester's house, Gwen was crying again. His parents were trying to feed her, but she was being fussy. He wished she could talk so she could tell his mom exactly what she wanted or what was wrong. He wondered how long it would be before she was able.

Sylvester sat at his desk, flipping a large silver dollar between his fingers. Over, under, over, under. He stared at a page in a book called *Secrets of Magic Tricks*. It was amazing how much work magic took. Solving mysteries was similar. Viola was really good at it. He was happy she had moved into the house across the yard from his. The Question Marks Mystery Club was fun. Having to pay attention—to remember little details, to think about their significance—made having to work at the diner less dreary. Recently, people in town had become so much more . . . mysterious.

Rosie was brushing her teeth in the upstairs bathroom when her sister Grace swung the door open. With a mouthful of toothpaste, Rosie threw Grace a dirty look, but she couldn't say anything if she didn't want to spray the mirror.

"You were taking too long," said Grace, who reached for her own toothbrush. "I have to get up early tomorrow for swim practice."

Rosie quickly spit, rinsed, and got out of the way. That's how it usually was in the Smitherses' house: crowded and annoying. She snuck quietly into the corner bedroom that she shared with Keira, her other sister. Greg and Stephen, her brothers, had the room next door. Grace was the only one with her own room, but she was already in high school and would probably be going to college in a couple of years.

Rosie couldn't imagine a time in which she would have her own room. She wondered what that might feel like. Peaceful? Or lonely?

She crawled into bed, thinking about the mysteries she and her friends had been playing with. Viola had upped the game tonight with the story she'd told about the missing dog. It was amazing, the secrets people kept. Why couldn't that husband just tell his wife how he felt? Rosie's family had always seemed able to do just that. Except . . . what if they hadn't? Rosie sat up, listening to the sounds of her family settling in downstairs, playing music, chatting with one another. How many secrets were they all keeping?

Hours later, Viola woke to a familiar sound.
Tap-tap-tap. Tap-tap-tap.
She clutched her sheets to her chin, chills pouring on her like ice water. She didn't know why this sound frightened her so much. Usually, she'd just figure out what was making it, and then everything would be okay. But it was hard to solve a mystery when the clues just weren't there.

She couldn't bring herself to throw back her covers and peek into the hallway. What if it *was* a ghost? Or worse . . . what if someone was there? Instead, she called to her parents.

Moments later, her father knocked on her bedroom door. Bleary-eyed, he peered in at her and said, "What's wrong?"

Viola wanted him to listen to the tapping sound that had woken her . . . but it had stopped. She wondered if her shouting had scared it away.

"Sorry," she said. "I thought I heard something."

Her father smiled. "Go to sleep, honey. Everything is fine." He closed her bedroom door.

But everything was not fine. There might be a ghost haunting her new house! If there was one thing Viola had learned recently, it was that when you needed an answer, you had to look for it. Rosie had mentioned that her mother was the town librarian. Maybe if Viola asked Rosie to help research the house's history, they would be a bit closer to figuring out these creepy nighttime sounds.

The group didn't meet for several days. Responsibility had finally caught up with them. Homework, sports, chores. Despite what they all wanted to believe, Moon Hollow was not *All Mysteries, All the Time*.

Still, Viola managed to convince Rosie to help her search the records at the library. With Mrs. Smithers's help, the girls discovered that Viola's house had not been owned by many people in the past century. The last owners, Mr. and Mrs. Denholm, had been a quiet couple from New York City who used the house mainly as a week-end escape. Before them, the house belonged to a woman named Fiona Hauptmann.

The girls gathered clues from the woman's obituary in the *Moon Hollow Herald*. Fiona had lived in the house her entire life. She'd inherited it from her parents, the Bransons, an old Hudson Valley family, when she was in her early twenties. The girls discovered a record that Fiona married soon after. Viola was intrigued by all the information, but it didn't seem to point toward anything supernatural or ghostly. She thanked Rosie and her mom for the help anyway.

When the whole group finally got together again, they'd managed to gather up a few mysteries. Rosie was excited to share hers first.

9

THE SNAPPED SNAKE
(A ???? MYSTERY)

"My mother's sister lives in Ohio," said Rosie. "Her family is like ours—huge. I have tons of cousins, but my favorite cousin is Bethany. She's my age exactly, and we talk on the phone all the time. We both really like animals—the weirder, the better.

"I was really excited to hear that Bethany had gotten a pet snake for her birthday last week. She named him Harry. He's light brown, about six inches long, and he lives in a terrarium in her bedroom. She told me that they blink at each other through the glass. She says she can tell what he's thinking, which is mostly about food. Her friends think Harry is gross, but Bethany doesn't think he's gross at all. She knows he's smart, and that's important to her.

"When Bethany called me yesterday afternoon, she was really upset. She said that something weird had just happened with Harry, and she wondered if I could help figure it out.

"What had happened was that Bethany's brother, Jasper, and his high-school friends were in her room checking out Harry. Bethany was in the kitchen getting an after-school snack, or else she would have kicked them out immediately. Anyway, she heard the boys start screaming, so she ran and found them crowded around the terrarium. Inside, Harry lay in several pieces, the front part of his body squirming around."

"Oh my gosh!" said Viola. "What happened to him?"

"You'll figure it out," said Rosie. "Terrified, Bethany demanded to know what they'd done to her snake. Jasper apologized, claiming that he and his friends had simply picked up Harry to play with him. But then the snake had begun to writhe around desperately. Before they knew what had happened, Harry had literally snapped!

"She examined Harry from behind the glass. He looked distraught and was trying to hide underneath a small piece of wood. But he was alive, despite the fact that his tail had shattered. Those pieces of him lay still.

"Bethany called me immediately, because her mom wasn't home yet to take Harry to the vet. I told her not to worry, that I didn't think Harry's life was in any danger. But I also told her that Harry wasn't exactly who she thought he was."

"What do you mean?" asked Sylvester.

"I told her that Harry isn't really a snake."
"Then what is he?" Sylvester continued.

"He's a lizard!"

"Really?" asked Sylvester. "A lizard that looks like a snake?"

Rosie nodded. "I've read that there is a kind of lizard called a glass snake. Despite their name, glass snakes aren't snakes at all—they're just lizards that don't have legs or feet! And something that Bethany said about Harry's behavior *before* the accident proved to me that he's a lizard. **What tipped me off?"**

"Bethany had told me that she and Harry blinked at each other through the glass. That is how they 'communicate.' Now, everyone who knows anything about reptiles will tell you that snakes cannot blink."

"Oh, sure," said Sylvester. "Who doesn't know that?"

"Don't tell me *you* knew that," said Woodrow, smirking.

"I might have known that," Sylvester answered, looking offended.

"Yeah, but you might *not* have."

Rosie sighed and continued. "But lizards can blink. And that was good news, because it meant that as soon as Harry calmed down a little bit, he would be fine."

"But he's still in pieces!" said Sylvester. *"How can Harry possibly be fine?"*

"When some lizards are in danger, they shed their tails to distract predators and escape from becoming a meal. When Jasper and his friends picked up Harry, the lizard felt threatened, and he broke his tail off to get away from them. And I guess it worked! Harry will grow another tail, even though it won't be as long as his first one. So ultimately, Harry will be fine . . . just a bit shorter than he was before. Bethany was a little weirded out, but totally relieved that her new friend is superpowered."

"Whoa," said Sylvester, "I wish I could regrow pieces of my body!"

"Why?" asked Viola, giving him a funny look. "Have you ever lost one?"

"No," he answered with a silly smile, "but I could try."

"Gross!" said Rosie. "Don't you dare."

After a moment, Woodrow spoke up. "Hey, you guys, I've got a good story too."

"Okay," said Viola, leaning forward. "Let's hear it."

10

THE CASE OF THE BIG BULLY
(A ???? MYSTERY)

"Kyle Krupnik is probably the shortest boy in our grade, and he's really quiet, but he's also really nice, so we've been friends ever since I moved here.

"Yesterday, after gym class, I saw Kyle in the locker room. I stopped to say hello and asked him why he'd sat out the game of kickball that period. He told me that he'd twisted his ankle during gym earlier in the week, but that the school nurse said he'd be okay if he rested for a few days. I asked him if he was ready for Mrs. Frankle's math quiz, because I was so totally *not*. He bent down and picked up his notebook from the bottom of his locker, explaining that he'd studied all night. He also assured me that I'd be fine, since I pay attention in class and take good notes.

"Then, Mickey Molynew came down the aisle and knocked into Kyle's shoulder, obviously on

78

purpose. Kyle banged his shin on the nearest bench. I knew it must have hurt, because those benches are bolted to the floor, but Kyle kept his cool. Still, Mickey shouted out, 'Watch where you're walking, nerd!' You all know Mickey, right?"

"I don't," said Viola, curious. "He's sounds like a jerk."

"You could say that," Woodrow said. "Mickey is like five times Kyle's size and sort of terrifying. He's always wearing these really bright Hawaiian shirts, as if he's daring you to make fun of him for it. He loves a fight."

"Once he gets you in his sights," said Sylvester, nodding, "it's a battle to the finish."

"Well, Mickey was searching for one," Woodrow continued. "And even though he scares me, I wasn't going to let him get away with picking on my friend.

"Kyle noticed how angry I was, so he grabbed my sleeve. 'Forget him. Coach Winslow can see us.' He nodded at the gym teacher's office door, which is right next to the locker room's entrance. 'If we fight, we'll get detention.' I was nervous that Mickey might try to shove Kyle into one of the tall lockers, like I'd seen him do to other kids. Then Mickey bolted out of there, so I figured we should too. But it wasn't over.

79

"In math class, just as Mrs. Frankle began passing out the quiz, Mickey told her that his textbook had been stolen after school the day before—and that one of his friends had seen Kyle breaking into his gym locker to swipe it from the top shelf. Mickey claimed that he hadn't been able to study for the quiz.

"Kyle turned strawberry red. When Mrs. Frankle asked him if that was true, Kyle whispered that he'd never steal anything from anyone.

"Mrs. Frankle doesn't know Mickey the way the rest of us do. I think she's blinded by his ridiculous Hawaiian shirts. So she had no way of knowing which of them was telling the truth. She finished handing out the quiz and told both of them that they could sort this whole problem out at the principal's office when they were finished.

"Mickey needed to have the last word. He asked, 'But I can make up the quiz once he gives me my book back, right, Mrs. Frankle?' She agreed that he could, if in fact Kyle had taken it in the first place. Kyle rolled his eyes, but then got to work.

"After class, when everyone had left the room, I went up to Mrs. Frankle and told her that I was certain I knew which of them was lying. *Do you know?"*

"It was Mickey, of course. Still, Mrs. Frankle just stared at me, as if she needed to know more before she could make any decisions. She wanted proof. *Where do you think I found it?*"

"In the locker room before class, I saw the inside of Kyle's locker. His stuff was piled at the bottom. The locker room lockers are different than the hall lockers. They're taller. Kyle had to bend down to pick up his math notebook. He's not tall enough to reach the shelf. Since Mickey accused Kyle of taking his textbook from the top shelf in his gym locker, I knew he must be lying.

"Mrs. Frankle crossed her arms. 'Kyle could easily have used the bench to climb to the top shelf,' she told me.

"'Not true,' I answered.

"*'Why not?' she asked.*

"'All the benches in the locker room are bolted to the floor,' I answered, 'so he couldn't have moved one over to the lockers.'

"Mrs. Frankle still wasn't happy. 'He might have jumped,' she said. I knew he hadn't, and I told her so. *'How can you be so sure?' she asked.*

"Kyle couldn't have jumped, because he hurt his ankle earlier that week. Besides, if Kyle had come back into the locker room after class was over, Coach Winslow would have noticed. His office is right next to the door.

"Mrs. Frankle was finally convinced. For her proof, all she needed to do was check with Coach Winslow, who confirmed that Kyle had not returned to the locker room before it had been locked up for the night.

"Kyle told me that Mrs. Frankle apologized to him, especially since he managed to get an A-minus on the quiz, even under all that pressure. Mickey, on the other hand, failed the quiz, was not allowed to retake it, and ended up in detention that afternoon. In fact, Kyle says that when the faculty checked Mickey's locker, the math textbook was sitting up on the top shelf, untouched . . . probably since the beginning of school.

"Just goes to show that if you're going to start accusing people of stealing your stuff, you better make sure that your stuff is actually missing."

11

THE MYSTERY OF THE
EARLY MORNING VANDAL
(A ? MYSTERY)

"That is amazing, Woodrow!" said Viola. "You solved the mystery *and* helped out your friend. That's what this is all about, isn't it?" Woodrow's smile grew extra-wide. "Hey, speaking of weird accusations, I've got another story.

"A couple nights ago, after dinner, my parents turned on the police scanner, and we listened to the strange reports people were calling in. I know it's an odd family activity, but my mom used to have to do that sort of thing for her job in Philly, and we all got into it. And you all know how much I like a good mystery." She laughed.

"One of the calls was a complaint from an elderly man about a suspicious car he'd noticed crawling really slowly through this neighborhood every morning, just before dawn. What the old man was doing up that early, he didn't say. But he did mention that whoever was driving this car was vandalizing his neighbors' houses."

"In this neighborhood?" said Sylvester.

Viola nodded. "He claimed that the driver was throwing heavy objects, possibly water balloons, which would smack into the front porches. The man was worried his house would be next. The police planned a stakeout the next morning.

"I decided to have a stakeout of my own. I set my alarm clock for super-early. I crawled out of bed before dawn, dug around in my detective kit, and pulled out the binoculars that my grand-parents got me for my ninth birthday—back when I thought I might want to be a spy, just like Harriet in those old books.

"I crawled downstairs, happy not to hear any eerie tapping noises. Then I crouched behind the loveseat near the front window, hiding just under the windowsill so I had a great view up and down the road.

"For a long time, nothing happened, and I struggled to keep my eyes open. I think I dozed off for a minute or two, but I jolted awake when I heard an engine puttering up the street. I peered up the hill just as that black car let out a big bang and disappeared over the horizon. Its noisy exhaust pipe was backfiring again. I still don't know who that car belongs to, but I'm dying to find out just so I can tell him to fix it!"

"I think I heard it again this morning too," said Rosie. "It woke me up and everything."

"So annoying!" Viola said. "Anyway, a few minutes later, the sun was just starting to peek over the horizon, and I was about to give up. But then I heard another car coming up the road. This one was a small blue hatchback. To my surprise, I saw the driver throw something hard out the window. The object flew across Rosie's yard and hit her front porch."

"It did?" Rosie said, sounding scared.

Viola nodded. "But the driver did the same thing again in front of my house. Suddenly, all thoughts of vandalism flew out of my head. The guy was only doing his job. *Do you have a clue who he was?*"

"It was the newspaper delivery guy. Some high-school kid with a route. In fact, he was delivering the *Moon Hollow Herald*, the paper my mom works for! The old man who had complained to the police was just being paranoid."

"What a weirdo!" said Woodrow.

"Don't be mean," said Rosie. "My grandparents get confused sometimes too. We all do, in fact."

"Sorry." Woodrow blushed. "But, hey, I've seen that black car driving around. It looks like that one Mr. Reynolds drove." He glanced at Viola. "He lived in that weird old house across the street from you."

"The car might have come from across the street," said Viola. "I could have missed it when I closed my eyes."

"Yeah," said Rosie. "But I thought that house was empty. My dad told me Mr. Reynolds died in there last year."

"Weird," said Viola. "Maybe someone else bought his car. Maybe they bought the house too."

"But there was never any For Sale sign out front," Rosie said, rubbing her arms, as if chilled.

"Speaking of strange cars," Sylvester added, "listen to this."

12

THE HOLE IN THE TRUNK
(A ?? MYSTERY)

"A few days ago, I was doing my homework at the diner counter when two teenagers, Derek and James, came in and sat down a few chairs away. Marjorie, our waitress, knows them pretty well and asked for their order, but they could barely stop their conversation to glance at her. Marjorie doesn't take nonsense from any of the customers, but she also can't pass up a bit of gossip, so she interrupted them and demanded to know what was so important that they couldn't even order their usual root beer floats. I, of course, listened in stealthily . . . if that's even a word."

"Technically," said Viola, "I think it is."

"Derek and James are next-door neighbors and best friends. They live up in the hills past Loon Lake. Whenever they come into the diner, they always seem to have something to argue about, like whose favorite team is going to win

89

the playoffs, or who's going to ask out Tamara Gillespie first, or which of them has a higher grade point average. They're always in competition."

"I know what that's like," said Rosie, thinking of her own siblings.

"Derek had just bought his first car—a used Buick. Big as a boat and bright green. He was really excited about it. Anyway, the morning before, Derek was woken by a massive boom from outside. It sounded like a gunshot or a cannon, he said."

"Hey, maybe that black car was driving around up there?" Woodrow suggested.

Sylvester shook his head. "You'd think so, but no. It was something completely different. Derek scrambled out of bed and raced out to the driveway where he'd parked his new car. When he saw it, he screamed. There was a huge, smoking hole punched all the way through the Buick's trunk. The back tires were flattened. He was certain that someone had vandalized the car.

"Furious, he ran across the yard and pounded on James's front door. James had already been woken up by the sound of the explosion, and once he answered the door, Derek accused James of being jealous of him having a car first. James freaked out, angry that Derek would even think he was capable of doing something like this.

"After Derek calmed down and came to his senses, he apologized. Then, together, they decided that they would find whoever did this . . . and they would destroy him."

"Yeah!" said Woodrow, rubbing his hands together.

"They examined every inch of the car, looking for clues, and figured that the only way the damage was even possible was by gunshot. But what kind of gun could punch a hole through a car?

"Finally, James looked at the driveway underneath the hole. To his surprise, he found a deep indentation in the asphalt itself, almost like a small crater. He instantly knew that this had not been caused by a gun. Inside the crater, James said he found the evidence to prove that, in fact, no one had vandalized the car. *Any clue what James found?*"

"James reached under the car and pulled out a fist-size, pockmarked piece of metal. It was warm to the touch. It didn't look like any sort of bullet or cannonball. In fact, they said it didn't look like anything they'd ever seen. At first they were confused. Passing the piece of metal back and forth, they began to comprehend their awesome situation."

"Where did the chunk of metal come from?" asked Rosie.

"Outer space! Based on the crater and the damage to the car, the boys believed that Derek was the victim of an extremely rare meteorite fall."

"Hey!" said Woodrow. "I watched a meteor shower from my bedroom window a few nights ago. There were a few really bright ones. Maybe that was when it happened."

"Wow, cool!" said Sylvester. "I wish I'd seen that. Anyway, the boys went back inside and did some research online. They found out that, in the past century, small meteorites had crashed through several other cars, and even some roofs!

"They called the police to report the accident. Since then, some scientists have already been up to their street to examine the damage. In fact, Derek says a museum offered to pay him for the meteorite . . . and for the car itself. He says he's thinking of using the money to buy a brand-new one."

"That's an amazing story," said Rosie. "Maybe we could all go up to the house and see if the crater is really there."

"I'm sure Derek wouldn't mind," said Sylvester. "He is a regular at the diner, after all."

That Saturday morning, the group rode their bikes up into the hills and found a crater nearly three feet in diameter in Derek's driveway. In the pavement, several giant cracks reached out from the center of the hole. It was as impressive as they'd hoped it would be. Derek came out of his house and, recognizing Sylvester, said hello with a look of pride that he had suddenly become a local celebrity.

The group didn't stay long. Woodrow and Sylvester were taking the train down to New York City that afternoon to meet up with Woodrow's father. They were staying the night. The next day, Mr. Knox was taking the boys to a comic book show.

While Woodrow and Sylvester were gone, the girls decided that they would hang out at Viola's house.

As it turned out, their weekends were quite eventful.

On Monday afternoon, at the Four Corners, the group had plenty to talk about.

13

THE MYSTERY OF THE GREEN MOOSE
(A ??? MYSTERY)

"After you guys left for the city," Viola began, "Rosie came over for lunch. It's a good thing she did, because we ended up helping my mom solve another crime."

"What?" said Woodrow. "Again?"

Rosie chuckled as Viola continued. "At the kitchen table, Mom was writing an article about a dispute between two local men. We asked her to explain the details, figuring that maybe we could help.

"Mr. Fredericks owns an antiques shop at the edge of town. My parents took me by there when we first moved here. You've probably seen the place. The building is an old barn, and there's a whole bunch of junk outside leaning against one of the walls near the gravel parking lot. Inside, there's real neat stuff—lots of old books and toys and furniture—piled right up to the rafters.

"So, last week, Mr. Klein, who runs a local dairy farm, happened to come into the shop. He noticed a moose-shaped, green-copper weather vane for sale. He approached Mr. Fredericks and told him that this very weather vane had once belonged to his grandfather, who had purchased it from an artisan way back in the nineteen thirties. The weather vane had sat atop the dairy barn on Klein's farm until several years ago, when someone had stolen it. Mr. Klein was really upset and demanded that Mr. Fredericks give it back.

"Mr. Fredericks refused, insisting that he himself had crafted the moose many years ago, but had kept it in storage. Only recently had he decided to sell it—so he reasoned that Mr. Klein had made a mistake. This was a different moose than the one that had been stolen from the dairy. When Mr. Klein began to argue, Mr. Fredericks accused him of making up the story about the theft in order to get the weather vane for free. Furious, Mr. Klein stormed out of the shop and went directly to the police, hoping that they could settle the matter.

"But the police told him that it was one man's word against the other's.

"My mom said it was an interesting story but told us that the case might never be settled because there really was no proof.

"Well, Rosie and I put our heads together, and after a while, we realized that there *was* proof. And we used it to figure out who was swindling who."

"Which man was telling the truth?" Rosie asked the boys.

"Mr. Klein's claim that the weather vane was stolen from the roof of his barn is the truth," said Viola. *"How did we know?"*

"The fact that the moose is made out of copper but was green proves that the moose spent a lot of time outside. Rosie explained to me that the copper had oxidized, which means a chemical reaction occurred that made the metal change to a greenish hue when it was exposed to water. Years of rain and snow while sitting on top of the dairy barn turned the moose the same color as the Statue of Liberty."

"So what does that prove?" asked Woodrow.

"Mr. Fredericks claimed that he'd kept the moose in storage since he'd crafted it himself a few years ago. If that was true, the moose would have been shiny and penny-colored. Since Mr. Fredericks obviously made up his story, we reasoned that he might have actually been the thief. We certainly had no proof of that, but my mom contacted Mr. Klein and told him how he could get his moose back. When Mr. Klein approached Mr. Fredericks again—this time armed with our argument—Mr. Fredericks gave in.

"To thank us, Mr. Klein gave us each a month's worth of farm-fresh dairy. Rosie and I are going to teach ourselves how to make ice cream. You guys can help too if you want."

The boys glanced at each other, then quickly nodded.

"Mint–chocolate chip, please," said Sylvester with his eyes wide.

14

THE MAGNIFICENT CASE OF THE McKENZIE COMIC (A ??? MYSTERY)

"How was your trip to New York?" Rosie asked Woodrow.

"It was fun," he said. "But Sylvester ran into a little bit of trouble at the comic book show."

Sylvester cleared his throat, as if preparing to perform. "I wouldn't say I *ran* into trouble. . . . I would say I *thwarted* it. My favorite comic book is called McKenzie the Magnificent. It's about a parlor magician who also happens to have secret superpowers. The story takes place during the Great Depression. McKenzie travels around the Dust Bowl with a medicine show, impressing and entertaining the poor people, and every now and again, vanquishing an evildoer or dastardly villain.

"Since the series started, two different people have written and drawn the books. Jerry Jones,

Senior, began the series in the forties, and recently his son, Jerry Jones, Junior, took over. I like both of them equally, but the older comics are much rarer. That makes them more popular at these kinds of shows, especially if they're signed.

"My mom and dad gave me a little bit of extra money to pay for food while I was staying with Mr. Knox, but Woodrow's dad insisted on treating us to everything. So I ended up with some cash to spend at the comic show on Sunday. I was excited to look for one of the older McKenzie books. I thought it would be a really cool souvenir.

"The convention hall was enormous. Every aisle was packed with people. It was hard to even see what everyone was waiting in line for. But we did end up seeing some amazing stuff. Like the Marvel preview table and the DC giveaways. We saw tons of costumed avengers. Someone had even dressed up like Jabba the Hut!

"Finally, I found a vendor who was selling McKenzie issues. One copy was prominently displayed. It was super old and a little bit worn out, but I looked closer and saw a signature scrawled across the cover. It read, 'Jerry Jones, Senior. September 25, 1950.' I checked the price and realized I could just afford it. I had to get it, even if it was beat up—the signature made it worthwhile. I asked Woodrow and his dad, and they both agreed it was totally cool.

"But just in time, I realized that I was about to waste my money. ***Do you know why buying the comic would be a waste?***"

"I looked closer at the signature and realized it was a forgery. I'd never seen Jerry Jones's autograph before, so I wasn't sure what it was supposed to look like. But something else about it tipped me off. *What was it?*"

"The fact that the autograph read 'Jerry Jones, Senior,' and was also dated nineteen fifty proved to me that the signature was a fake. *Why?*"

"Jerry Jones, Senior, would not have signed his name as 'Senior' back then because he wouldn't have had to distinguish himself from his son, who hadn't even been born yet.

"All of a sudden, the situation just seemed really sketchy, so I put the comic book back and returned my parents' money to my pocket.

"I left the comic book show empty-handed, but I still had a great time. I know that one day I'll be able to find a real signed copy of McKenzie the Magnificent, and it will be totally awesome."

"Wow," said Viola. "You should have reported the vendor for trying to sell you fake merchandise."

"Yeah, I thought about it," Sylvester replied. "But I don't know for sure if the guy who was trying to sell the book even knew it was junk. He might have been just as clueless as I'd been when I took out my money."

"Hmm," said Rosie. "You never know when people might be trying to trick you. Someone in my own family tried to put one over on me just last night!"

1⁵

THE MYSTERY OF THE MISSING ASPARAGUS (A ??? MYSTERY)

"Sunday dinners are a big deal at my house," Rosie continued. "It's the only time of the week that my parents make all my brothers and sisters and me sit down at the table for a meal together. Everyone has a job to do, whether it's grocery shopping, or cooking, or setting the table, or doing the dishes. We usually switch off each chore.

"Yesterday, Greg and Keira did the shopping. My mom gave them a list and they went to the store in the afternoon. Mom and Stephen did most of the cooking, even though I helped chop the onions because I like to see how long I can last before the fumes make me start to cry. At the last minute, Dad came in from his office and set the table. After dinner, Grace and I planned on cleaning up.

"We sat down, ready to eat my mom's famous

meat loaf when she shouted out, 'Wait! We're missing a dish! Where's the roasted asparagus?' Looking confused, my father said, 'I set the table, but I didn't see any asparagus dish.'

"I rushed to the kitchen to grab the extra plate, but the counter was empty. I called back to the dining room to let everyone know there was nothing else to serve. I started to wonder if we might have our own mystery on our hands.

"'I'm sure we put the asparagus on the ceramic blue serving tray,' Mom said. Stephen agreed.

"I decided to stay in the kitchen to look for clues. First, I checked the oven, to see if the veggies were still in there. When I opened the door, a waft of warm air blew against my face, but the oven was empty. It had been on, but that didn't prove anything, because the meat loaf had been baked.

"Next, I checked the refrigerator to make sure someone hadn't accidentally put the tray in there to chill. But the asparagus were nowhere to be found. In the dishwasher, I noticed my mother's ceramic blue serving tray, rinsed clean and tucked away at the rear. If the tray was now clean, I suddenly had a hunch where I'd find the asparagus.

"Where do you think I looked next?"

"I checked the garbage can. When I lifted the lid, I found a pile of steaming greens, freshly seasoned and looking completely unappetizing. I called to my mom, and when she came and saw the bin, she screamed.

"Mom went back into the dining room and claimed that one of my brothers or sisters must have sabotaged the dish because they never like to eat their vegetables. She went around the table asking each of us why we would do such a thing, but no one took responsibility. She said that if the guilty party didn't fess up, she wouldn't serve us dessert ever again. A most extreme threat, but still, no one said a word.

"My mother sat back down, shaken up by our betrayal. My dad, who hates any sort of drama, spoke up. He said, 'It's a real shame that someone would think to do such a thing, since the asparagus sauce looked so delicious and your mother worked so hard.'

I looked around the table, trying to see if I could figure out which of my siblings had done it simply by reading their expressions. But they all looked the same: annoyed.

"I glanced around the table one last time, and slowly, the answer came to me. I knew the culprit. ***Do you?***"

"Trying not to sound sheepish, I spoke up. 'Dad, if you thought the sauce looked so delicious, then why did you toss the asparagus in the garbage?' His mouth dropped open, along with everyone else's. I didn't mean to sound disrespectful, but the way my dad looked at me proved to me that I was right. *How had I known?*"

"Dad had first claimed that he hadn't seen any asparagus dish when he was setting the table. Then, after my mom had finished scolding us, he added that it was a shame someone had tossed it, since the sauce looked so good. He wasn't around when Mom was cooking dinner, and he hadn't gotten up from the table to look in the garbage. Therefore, he never should have *seen* the sauce . . . unless he was the one who had dumped it out to begin with. Confronted, he had to admit what he'd done. His excuse? He hates asparagus.

"My mother was furious with him, but my siblings were even angrier that he tried to blame us. He knew he would have to do some serious damage control if he were to escape the dining room alive. So he announced that after dinner, he'd drive us all out to the ice cream parlor at the mini-golf course for hot fudge sundaes. Also, he promised to eat all his vegetables next time, or at least let us know if he didn't feel like it. It was funny to realize that my parents aren't perfect.

"When we got back home from the golf course, my brothers and sisters all congratulated me for catching him in the act. So many times, I feel like I'm invisible in that house. It felt good to actually be recognized. My oldest sister, Grace, even let me brush my teeth first before bed."

*1*6

THE BEAST IN THE RIVER
(A ?? MYSTERY)

A few weeks into September, the summer warmth returned. One Saturday morning, from her bedroom window, Viola watched a number of boaters reveling on the river. The buzzing of the engines sounded like cicadas. It made her think of another sound. She hadn't heard the tapping from the basement in a while and wondered if it had stopped for good.

When she went downstairs for breakfast, her mother was sitting at the table, writing in a notebook and drinking from a steaming coffee mug. Noticing her daughter, Mrs. Hart lit up. "Honey," she said, "I've got some exciting news."

Moments later, after quick phone calls to the others, Viola met Rosie, Sylvester, and Woodrow outside. Before any of them could ask her what this was all about, Viola blurted out, "There's a beast in the river."

"A beast?" said Sylvester, wearing an expression of horror.

"What kind of beast?" Rosie asked, looking more skeptical than frightened.

"A huge serpent," said Viola, with a dramatic flourish of her arms. "Mom said that people have been calling in sightings to the newspaper for decades. Some say it's long and green with flaming red eyes, and it twists its body as it hunts along the shore. Others claim that they've seen it farther out in the middle of the river, poking its narrow head just above the waves, spewing water from its nostrils. And one person says the thing knocked up against his boat, nearly capsizing it. This year is the fortieth anniversary of the first sighting."

"I've heard about this before," said Woodrow. "My mom gets all kinds of monster-sighting calls at the park service in the mountains. It's pretty common. The monster always turns out to be an upturned tree root or a rock or something completely normal."

"Well," said Viola, "my mom told me that the *Herald* is holding a contest for the anniversary. They made the announcement in this morning's paper. Whoever can provide the best photographic proof that this beast actually exists will get a cash prize—and they'll also be allowed to name the creature! The *Herald* plans on printing the picture of the winner and the beast side by side, right on the front page."

"We have to win!" said Sylvester. "*This* is what we do!"

"Does anyone have a camera?" asked Rosie.

Woodrow nodded. "My dad got me a great one for my birthday last year. It has a mega-zoom lens."

"Cool," said Viola. "What are you guys doing this afternoon?"

After lunch, the group followed the road down the hill, past the train tracks, and to the edge of the Hudson River, armed with Woodrow's camera and Viola's notebook. Rosie had brought several empty glass vials with cork stoppers in case she needed to collect water specimens. And Sylvester carried a leftover loaf of bread from his family's diner for bait.

They spent the day watching the waves and complaining to one another how unfair it was that they didn't have a boat. Rosie reasoned that all of the activity in the water would frighten any animal away—especially an ultra-secretive, mysterious beast-type thing. Still, Sylvester continued to break off pieces of bread and toss them toward the shoals at the water's edge, while Woodrow sat with his camera, ever-ready, snapping pictures of everything that moved. Most of the shots turned out to be of garbage floating by in the current—paper cups, a soda can, a bag of chips—all blown off the boats by the wind.

By the time the sun began to set, their disappointment had grown. Before they said good-bye for the night, Viola reminded them that they still had another day before returning to school. But Sunday went even quicker than Saturday, and they were just as unsuccessful.

On Monday after school, Viola learned from her mom that the newspaper had awarded someone the prize. Dr. Helmut Blunt, a professor of biology and a colleague of her father's at Moon Hollow College, was fishing off the Grand Street Dock when he hooked what he thought was a large pike. The fish was so heavy, the old man claimed, that his reel had bent at a sharp angle. He struggled for a short time, when suddenly the line broke and he flew backward, landing next to his gear. He heard splashing sounds under the dock, and when he peeked over the edge, he saw something he'd never imagined seeing. Aware of the contest, he'd brought his camera, so he quickly snapped several pictures. When Mrs. Hart showed them to Viola, she gasped in horror.

"Whoa," said Rosie, passing the paper to Woodrow. "That is a really bizarre-looking creature. I've never seen anything like it."

"He's so ugly!" Woodrow said, squinting at the grainy image. In the photograph, a reptilian snout with a gaping mouth came up out of the water toward the camera, its teeth filled with the flesh of its stolen prey, its wide eyes seeming to glow.

"Who?" answered Sylvester. "Dr. Blunt or the beast?"

"Don't be mean," said Viola, taking back her copy of the newspaper. "The man won fair and square."

Several days had passed since the Question Marks had learned that they'd lost the contest. That morning, the Herald released Dr. Blunt's photo as well as the name he had invented for the creature: *The Hudson River Oftrem Snake*. After school, they'd met behind their houses once again, this time not as detectives, but merely as friends.

"What kind of name is *that*?" said Sylvester.

"I would have called him Moonie the Monster or something that actually makes sense."

"*Moonie the Monster* makes sense?" Woodrow teased.

"In the article," Rosie interrupted, "Dr. Blunt explains that he developed the name from the genus and species names of some river snakes."

"Is the word *oftrem* Latin?" Viola asked.

"Not that I could find," said Rosie. "I searched for it on the Internet. In fact, I don't even think the word *oftrem* exists. I'm pretty sure he made it up." She paused, reaching for the newspaper once again. Glancing at it, she said, "Hmm, I wonder if that means he made up the photo too."

"But it looks so real," said Woodrow.

"Maybe we just *want* it to look real," Viola suggested. "It's exciting to believe in the beast, isn't it?"

"There was a famous picture of the Loch Ness Monster that looked real too," Sylvester said, "but that one was a bunch of baloney. The guy who shot it said so. . . . Well, eventually."

"If there's one thing we've learned as a mystery club," said Viola, "it's that we can't go around accusing people of stuff they didn't do. We need proof that Dr. Blunt made it up."

"But how?" said Rosie. "Isn't the fact that he invented a nonsense name enough?"

"Not really," said Woodrow, thinking. "But maybe we're wrong about the name. Maybe it isn't nonsense."

"What do you mean?" asked Viola.

"Maybe he chose those words for a reason."

"Like what?" said Sylvester. "You think he was trying to tell everyone something? Like by code?"

"Not by code," said Woodrow. "But something like it."

"What do you mean?" asked Rosie.

"I think maybe Dr. Blunt's name for the beast is an anagram," said Woodrow.

"What's an anagram?" asked Sylvester.

"We learned the term in class last year," said Rosie. "Remember? An anagram is a word or words whose letters can be moved around to make other words."

"Like a puzzle," Woodrow said, nodding.

"I think you guys could be right," said Viola, opening her notebook. "Brilliant." She tore out several sheets of paper and handed them to the others. "If we're going to figure this out, we'd better get started now. There are a lot of letters here. And this might be the only way to prove that Dr. Blunt is up to something."

A long while later, the group was frustrated.

"I can't make sense of this," said Rosie, finally. *"The Hudson River Oftrem Snake* has too many letters!"

"Hold on," Woodrow answered. "You're right, Rosie. There *are* too many letters. But what if we don't use all of them?"

"Isn't the point to use all of the letters?" Sylvester asked.

"Try using *Oftrem Snake*," said Woodrow. After a few minutes, he gasped. "It worked! I got it. **Did you?**"

119

Viola gasped too. "If you rearrange the letters of *Oftrem Snake*, it becomes *Monster Fake!*" she said.

"Wow," said Sylvester. "*The Hudson River Monster Fake*. Or *Fake Monster*. That's actually kind of cool."

"I can't believe someone would do this to us," said Rosie, her mouth agape. "To the town."

"I can," Viola said, crossing her arms. "Now the question is: What are we going to do about it?"

"I don't think we should go to the paper," said Woodrow. "Dr. Blunt works with your father, right, Viola? We don't want to cause any trouble."

"Oh, *I* want to cause trouble," she said softly. "Or at least find out what the doctor was thinking."

"We could send him a letter," Rosie suggested. "Tell him we figured out his trick."

"That sounds like a good plan," said Viola.

They decided Woodrow should write it, since he was the one who had decoded the anagram first. After looking up Dr. Blunt's address online, he dropped the letter in the mail. Then, they waited.

A few days later, Woodrow slipped notes into

each of his friends' lockers, asking them to meet him at lunch. He had something to tell them.

When they had all met in the cafeteria at a long booth near the windows, he began. "Dr. Blunt called me last night." The group gasped, and Woodrow continued. "He actually congratu- lated us on figuring out his hoax."

"He congratulated us?" Viola couldn't believe it. She'd been so sure that he would have been upset or embarrassed at being caught.

"He told me that he doesn't believe that there's a beast in the river, but plenty of animals do live in the Hudson River—and the contest was actually really destructive to their habitat. People were trampling the shores, going out on their boats, disrupting the water, and polluting the river. Remember all the litter we saw that weekend?"

"So Dr. Blunt wanted the contest to be over as soon as possible?" guessed Rosie.

"Exactly," said Woodrow. "He found a rubber monster mask, half submerged it under the Grand Street Dock, and took pictures. And now he wants me to go to the paper and tell them what we discovered."

"Why would he want us to do that?" Sylvester asked.

"His plan backfired. Since the photo was printed, more and more people are on the river, hoping to catch a glimpse of the monster. And that's putting real animals in danger—including a creature that might account for the sightings of a 'beast.' It's an animal that he says needs to be protected by conservationists . . . people like my mom in the park service."

"Did Dr. Blunt say what kind of creature is actually in the river?" asked Viola.

"I think I know what it could be," said Rosie. "I've read about a fresh-water fish that lives in the Hudson River. It can grow really big. It's called a sturgeon."

"Exactly!" Woodrow said. "Dr. Blunt said a sturgeon is a kind of non-scaly, bottom-feeding fish that can grow several feet long—sometimes even longer than a human is tall. They're in danger, supposedly, because they produce eggs that people like to eat."

"Eww!" Sylvester exclaimed, dropping his tuna-salad sandwich onto his napkin.

"So what do we do?" Rosie asked.

"Contact the paper, like Dr. Blunt said. He wants to bring attention to the plight of the sturgeon here in Moon Hollow, and he hopes that this controversy will open people's eyes to the problem. He also wants to donate the money he won to the River Ecology Project, if the *Herald* lets him keep the prize."

Viola was quiet for a few seconds. "It's funny," she said. "After we learned that Dr. Blunt had faked the picture, I thought of him as the bad guy. But now, he seems like a pretty good guy."

"Yeah," Sylvester agreed, "makes you wonder: Who are the real beasts in the river?"

17

MOON HOLLOW GHOST STORIES

During lunch the next week, Sylvester and Woodrow approached Viola and Rosie, who were sitting together in their favorite booth near the cafeteria window. "Hey, Viola," Sylvester said, "what's going on with the ghost in your house? Have you heard any more strange noises?"

"Not lately," Viola answered, after chewing and swallowing a chunk of apple. "Why? You look like you've seen a ghost yourself."

Woodrow shook his head. "We just heard some kids saying that the old Reynolds house is haunted too."

"The creepy place across the street from us?" Rosie said, surprised. She turned toward Viola. "Mr. Reynolds was the guy who owned that old black car—the one you and Woodrow have seen driving around."

"Right," said Viola, picturing the house in her

mind. The building sat up the hill away from the street, hidden by a tangle of trees and vines. It was covered in formerly white wooden shingles. The paint was faded now, the grass overgrown. She guessed that's what happened when an owner died and his property fell into ruin. It was sad, really. If any house in this town was likely to be haunted, that was the one, even more so than her own. "So why do people think the place is haunted . . . other than the fact that it's a total creep-fest?"

Sylvester pointed across the cafeteria. "Ricky Farrell said he was riding his bike late last week and saw a light floating inside a few of the upstairs windows."

"That doesn't mean the place is haunted," said Rosie. "Does it?"

"Obviously not," Viola answered. "Still, why would someone be sneaking around in an abandoned place? I remember Rosie mentioned that no one's bought it since Mr. Reynolds died, right?"

"Yeah," said Woodrow. "It's still got all his stuff in it, I think."

"There you go!" said Viola. "Maybe it was a burglar. There could be valuables still in the house."

"Except that's not the only reason people are saying it's haunted," Sylvester continued. "They're claiming to have seen Mr. Reynolds."

"Where?" Rosie asked.

"In his yard, for one," Woodrow said. "He used to do a lot of gardening out there."

"And someone else said they actually saw him in town late one night," Sylvester added. "Just walking down the street, looking as alive as you and me."

"Wait a second," Viola said. "Couldn't it have been someone who just looked like Mr. Reynolds? People see what they want to see sometimes."

"You've never seen *this* guy, Viola," said Woodrow. "He looked like no one else. He was tall and thin, with a body like a scarecrow. He always wore a wide-brimmed straw hat and oversized jeans that he held up with bright red suspenders, like it was his uniform or something."

"That does sound pretty distinctive," Viola admitted.

"He kept to himself when he was alive," said Sylvester. "No one knew much about him."

Viola remembered the research she and Rosie had done about the previous owners of her own house. "Then we should find out about him

126

ourselves," she said. "I mean, two haunted houses right across the street from each other? What are the chances of that?"

"Maybe Moon Hollow is just filled with ghosts," said Sylvester, drawing up his eyebrows.

"Or maybe," said Viola, "we've got ourselves another mystery to solve."

*1*8

THE BLACK CAR CLUE
(A ?????? MYSTERY)

The group took turns that week staking out the Reynolds place after school. Viola and Rosie had the best view, since both of their houses faced uphill. But neither of them witnessed anyone going in or out. The house was completely silent. Viola creeped herself out by wondering if someone or something inside might be watching them too.

Then they all tried the library, just like Viola had done when she had read about Fiona Hauptmann, to see if they could learn more about the man who had once lived across the street from her. The library didn't have nearly as much information about Mr. Reynolds. A picture showed him exactly as Woodrow had described him: old, frail, but with a piercing, almost frightening stare. The group learned that before he'd retired, Nelson Reynolds had worked at a nearby prison as a late-shift guard. He had owned his house for a long time—fifty years at least. Again, none of their findings gave them a clue whether or not he had returned from beyond the grave. *But then*, wondered Viola, *what would?*

The next day, Woodrow came up with a new idea, which he mentioned to the group at lunch. "What if we try and look closer?"

"That's what we've been doing," said Rosie. "Paying attention, like Viola said on the day she moved in."

Woodrow shrugged. "I was thinking about looking even closer than we have before."

"You mean . . . ?" Viola tried to draw it out of him.

"He means trespassing," said Sylvester.

"What?" said Rosie. "No way."

"But if the house doesn't belong to anyone," Woodrow said, "then we're not really trespassing, right?"

"Just tell yourself that when you're sitting behind bars," Viola said.

"All I'm saying," Woodrow continued, "is that maybe we should check out the house. At the very least, we can walk up the driveway. If anyone asks us what we're doing, we can come up with an excuse. Isn't that what detectives do?"

"I guess we could say we're lost," Rosie said.

"Or that we're selling candy bars for the basketball team," Sylvester chimed in.

"Or that we're ghost hunters!" Woodrow said.

"Or that we're just kids who didn't know any better," Viola suggested. "Although that's totally not going to fly if my parents find out what we're up to."

"So it's settled, then," said Woodrow. "After school, we meet in front of the Reynolds house to do some exploring."

The day had clouded over, and the wind was rising, sweeping dead leaves across the dried-out lawns of the neighborhood. As the kids stood on the sidewalk across the street from the over-grown tangle of trees, they felt the first truly cold blast of autumn. Viola clutched at herself, wondering if it was merely the weather which was giving her chills.

Woodrow led the way up the cracked asphalt driveway and into the shadowy tunnel of over-hanging branches. Ahead, a small garage sat detached from the rest of the house. Woodrow whipped out his camera and began taking pictures. Viola opened her notebook, prepared to jot down anything she noticed that might be important. Rosie knelt on the driveway, examining what looked like some sort of stain. Oil perhaps? And Sylvester approached the house, feeling along its foundation, as if he might come across a secret entrance.

"Hey, you guys," Woodrow whispered. "Check this out." He was peering through the dirty window of the garage's side door. He held up his camera and pressed the shutter, and a flash lit up the surrounding trees.

"Careful," said Viola. "We don't want to draw too much attention."

"Sorry," Woodrow answered, "but I thought I saw something inside the garage, and I needed a bit of light."

"What did you see?" Sylvester asked, coming up close behind him.

"A car."

The girls raced to catch a glimpse as well. "What kind of car?" Rosie asked. But before Woodrow could answer, Sylvester had turned the doorknob, and they all found themselves staring into the dim space beyond.

"I guess you can see for yourself now," said Woodrow, stepping inside.

"Wait!" Viola called. Even though this was thrilling, something was holding her back. "This could be a bad idea. What if someone's watching us?"

"Like who?" said Sylvester, following Woodrow into the garage.

"Like . . . Mr. Reynolds."

Rosie took a deep breath, then she too disappeared into the shadows. Woodrow called out, "Well, I guess if he *is* watching, then we can just ask him why he's haunting this place. Case closed."

Viola closed her eyes and thought to herself, *I've created monsters*, before stumbling forward into the darkness. Once her eyes adjusted, she noticed her friends standing around the front of a large black car, staring in wonder. "This is Mr. Reynolds's old car," said Sylvester. "I remember him driving this thing everywhere."

"Did it ever backfire?" Viola asked, reaching out and brushing dirt from the warm hood. Her hand came away filthy.

"You mean like the one we've heard recently?" Woodrow said. "I think so."

"Do ghosts drive cars?" Rosie said.

"Maybe what we've been hearing was a ghost car," whispered Sylvester. "Maybe the ghost version of Mr. Reynolds is driving a ghost version of his old car."

Viola shook her head. "No . . . the car we've seen recently—the one that keeps making all that noise—is no ghost. It's as solid as the car in front of us. The proof is right here."

"Where?" asked Woodrow.

"When I touched the car just now, the hood was warm. It's too cold out for the car to stay warm on its own, so that means someone has been driving this car today."

"Whoa," said Sylvester, reaching out and touching the hood himself. "You're right."

"But wouldn't we have seen someone pull up the driveway?" Rosie asked.

"Not if we were at school," said Viola.

Woodrow suddenly went rigid. "You guys. Do you know what that means?" No one answered. The look on Woodrow's face kept them silent. "Whoever drove this car might be in the house right now. He might have watched us come in here." The group turned toward the door, which was still open at the side of the garage. "What if he doesn't just call the police? What if he does something worse?"

"Shh! What was that?" said Rosie, flinching and stepping closer to Woodrow.

"I hear it too," said Viola. "Listen."

The sound of footsteps approached from outside, moving slowly, tentatively. Viola's heart raced as a shadow moved in front of the door. Before she could even think to hide, a figure appeared there, and Viola had to hold back a scream.

"Viola Hilary Hart," said her mother, "get out of there right this instant."

"Sorry, Mrs. Hart," said Woodrow, stepping forward. "It was my idea. We were trying to solve a mystery."

"What a big surprise," Mrs. Hart answered, waving them forward. "I suppose breaking and entering was part of this mystery? Come on, guys, out. Let's go." Once they were all standing on the driveway, she led them back toward the street. "I was home early, listening to the police scanner when I heard that someone had called in, claiming to have witnessed a group of four kids going somewhere they weren't supposed to be. When they mentioned the address, I knew who they were talking about. Now if we all run, maybe we can make it back across the street before the patrol cars arrive."

Thoroughly embarrassed, Viola sat with her friends at the Four Corners. It was cold and dark and the lawn was damp.

"Hey, at least it was your mom," Woodrow said, trying to ease the tension. "It could have been worse."

"Yeah, but now she made us promise that we won't go back up there again. She won't even go and knock on the door for us. How are we going to solve the mystery?"

Rosie raised her hand. "Remember the day we met Viola, how we figured out where she lived before she moved to Moon Hollow? I managed to find a similar clue while we were in the garage. I think it might actually help us figure out who's been driving that car. . . . I mean, if it's not the ghost of Mr. Reynolds. *Can you guess what I found in the garage?*"

Rosie pulled out a piece of scrap paper from her back pocket, and passed it around the small circle. "I wrote down the car's license plate. It's registered in New Hampshire, not here in New York State. I wonder if there's a way we can find out who it belongs to."

"So you *don't* think it's Mr. Reynolds's car?" said Sylvester.

"It looks like his car. Maybe he had a secret house in New Hampshire," Rosie said. "We need to find out, but how?"

"My dad has some friends in the New York State Police," Woodrow offered. "I wonder if he could ask them to run the plates."

"That would be so cool!" said Viola, happy not to have to make another trip up the creepy Reynolds driveway. This way, she wouldn't risk getting grounded—a punishment she could not afford right now.

Before they said good-bye, Woodrow promised he would call his father as soon as he got home. In the meantime, the two girls decided to keep watch on the house across the street, to see if anyone came or went.

Viola stayed up late that night. While her parents watched television in the family room, she hid in the living room, beneath the windowsill, the one that faced north toward the Reynolds house. She struggled to stay awake, mesmerized by the night, the wind, and the occasional passing car. Eventually, Viola's father discovered her and made her go upstairs to bed.

That night, she dreamt about gunshots, balloons popping, and firecrackers. When she woke in the morning, she realized that whoever was driving the black car must have left in the middle of the night. Its bad muffler had invaded her dreams.

"My dad got us a name," said Woodrow on Saturday, plopping down on the lawn in the backyard. "And you're never going to believe it."

"Oh, just tell us!" said Sylvester, joining him. The girls knelt and listened, growing impatient as Woodrow slowly unfolded a Post-it note.

"The car is registered to a man named Victor Reynolds. He lives in North Conway, New Hampshire."

"*Victor* Reynolds?" said Viola. "That's weird. He's got the same last name as Nelson Reynolds."

The kids all looked at one another, confused.

"Yeah," said Woodrow, smiling slightly, enjoying this. ***"Can you think of a reason?"***

"They've got to be related," said Rosie. "Could they be father and son? Cousins? Uncle and nephew?"

"But people have claimed to see Nelson Reynolds since his death. Maybe Nelson and Victor look exactly the same," Viola said. "Maybe they're brothers."

"Twin brothers," Woodrow added, nodding. "My mom's sisters are twins. They dress in similar clothes, right down to the same brand of shoe. Not all twins act like that, but enough of them seem to fit the pattern that it makes sense Victor and Nelson did the same. People thought they were seeing Mr. Reynolds around town because they *were* seeing him. Just the *wrong* Mr. Reynolds."

"So the house across the street isn't haunted at all?" said Viola. Maybe there was still hope that hers wasn't haunted either. But how to prove it?

"Nope," said Woodrow. "It sure doesn't seem that way."

"So what has Victor been doing in Nelson's house?" Sylvester asked.

"If you think about it," said Rosie, sitting up on her heels, "it's simple, really. ***Can you guess?***"

"If Nelson's car is registered to his brother, Victor," said Rosie, "that means Victor must have inherited it when Nelson died. Since there was never a For Sale sign at the house across the street, it makes sense that Victor inherited the house as well. Obviously, he's no ghost. He's probably just trying to clean up the place. Maybe he wants to move in. Or maybe he's preparing to sell it."

"I bet you're right," said Viola, a little disappointed. "I was sort of hoping, if not a ghost, we'd at least meet some burglars."

"Maybe next time," said Sylvester, reaching out and patting her shoulder.

October came quickly, and even though the Question Marks Mystery Club had discovered that a mere man had been "haunting" the house across the street, they were still having spooky thoughts. Halloween was approaching, and they needed to plan their costumes. They were considering going as characters from *The Wizard of Oz*.

It turned out that Victor Reynolds had in fact been preparing to sell the old house. Not long after the group's last meeting, he had placed an ad in the *Moon Hollow Herald*. A few days later, the long-awaited For Sale sign finally appeared, stuck into the overgrown lawn near the street.

From the sign peered the determined eyes of a sharp-faced woman. Her blond hair was pinned up on top of her head in an elaborate crisscrossing braid. Underneath the picture was a line of text that read, *For a Showing, Call Betsy Ulrich, Moon Hollow's Most Trusted Realtor.*

They hadn't seen the black car in weeks and figured Victor had probably gone back to New Hampshire for good, hiring Betsy to do the rest of the work for him. Viola thought they'd probably freaked him out the day they'd walked up his driveway and into his garage—enough so that he'd never want to come back!

To her disappointment, the mysteries had slowed ever further. Not even listening to the police scanner gave Viola any tips worth investigating. Then, at the end of the second week in October, to both her delight and horror, Viola finally heard the mysterious sounds in her house again.

It was an early evening, and her parents were both stuck late at work. She was sitting at the kitchen table, doing her homework, and there it was—the sound, slightly different than before. Now it was a *bang-bang-bang.* Goose bumps raced across her body, and Viola pulled her feet up off the floor, as if that would save her from any ghostly danger.

Viola immediately reached for the phone, which sat on the table, not far from her math textbook. She called her friends and asked if they could come right away. Minutes later, after dashing up the front hallway, Viola met Rosie, Sylvester, and Woodrow on the front porch.

"She's here again," said Viola. Then, realizing that they had no idea what she was talking about, she added, "Fiona Hauptmann. My ghost. Listen." She invited the group inside. As they stood in the foyer, the sound came again, banging and echoing up from under the floor.

"What's she doing down there?" asked Sylvester.

Rosie shushed him. "We don't want to scare her away."

"Quick," said Woodrow, heading toward the kitchen. "Where's that flashlight we used last time we went into the basement?"

"The basement?" said Viola. "We can't go *down* there." Woodrow turned back to look at her, shocked. And that was all it took for her to follow him.

Slowly, they opened the basement door and peered into the darkness. Mr. Hart still hadn't gotten around to fixing the light socket. The flashlight Viola had collected from her detective kit gave off some illumination, but not much. Woodrow held it, swinging it forward as he carefully made his way down. The others followed. At the bottom of the stairs, the banging came, it seemed, from all around them. The group clung to one another in fear. After a few seconds, the sound stopped, and they managed to let go, breathing deeply.

"What is going on down here?" asked Sylvester.

"Yeah," said Woodrow. "If it *is* the ghost of Fiona Hauptmann, why's she making so much noise?"

"Can I see the flashlight for a second?" Rosie asked. Woodrow handed it to her. As she made her way across the room, the group stayed close by. None of them wanted to touch the pure darkness. "Look up," she said. "The pipes and wires . . . Some of them lead toward the front of Viola's house." The group followed the pipes until they met the wall, where the large wooden shelving unit stood. "There. The wires go right behind those shelves. At the top."

Woodrow began, "You don't think—"

But Viola ignored him by stepping forward. She examined the side of the unit and gasped. Turning back to the group, she whispered, "There are hinges here."

"Wouldn't that mean that these shelves . . . are a door?" asked Sylvester, his eyes nearly popping out of his skull.

"Try it, Viola," said Rosie.

Pulling on the opposite side of the shelving unit, Viola managed to drag it forward several inches, the hinges screaming at her to stop. Then she noticed a small dark gap behind the shelves. "You guys, there's a hole here. A passageway."

BANG-BANG-BANG!

The group ran into one another, trying to get back to the stairs, but they tripped and fell and lay there tangled and unable to move until the noise finally stopped again.

"What are we going to do?" asked Viola, after a few moments of quiet. "I can't go in there." They all sat still, listening to the new silence, waiting for the sounds to come again.

"Well, we can't stop now," said Woodrow. "If you won't go, then I'll do it by myself."

"I'm with you, dude," said Sylvester.

Rosie looked at Viola, but she didn't need to say a word for her to understand. Finally, Viola said, "Oh, all right. But if I die, my parents are going to be *really* mad at you."

The boys struggled with the shelves, yanking hard, until the group was staring into a deep, dark tunnel. "If that banging sound comes again

144

right now, I really might just run back upstairs," said Sylvester.

Woodrow pointed the light forward, and they all had a better view of what lay inside. The ghostly light illuminated what appeared to be a narrow corridor. The walls were made of ancient-looking stone, and the ceiling was pitched, like doorways in old churches. The pipes and wires that Rosie had noticed continued down the passage along the ceiling, held up with small rusted hooks. Every few feet, the wires drooped where an empty light socket hung. "Check it out," said Rosie. "Someone must have once used this tunnel a lot. It even had its own lighting system."

"Too bad there aren't any lightbulbs hooked up now," said Sylvester.

"Come on," Woodrow said. "Let's go."

And in they went. They stayed close together, as if someone or something might suddenly come whooshing out of the darkness to attack. After walking several feet, they noticed the floor begin to slant upward at a slight angle. In the front, Woodrow crunched glass beneath his sneaker. "One of the lightbulbs," he whispered. "Be careful."

Eventually, they came to the end—what appeared to be a solid wooden wall. "Strange," said Rosie. "What now?"

Woodrow reached out and knocked quietly on the wall. *Tap-tap-tap.* The sound echoed up and down the tunnel behind them.

"Hey!" Viola said, exclaiming quietly. "That was just like the sound I heard from my bedroom at night. A tapping noise."

The kids all stared at one another, as if an answer was slowly materializing before them. "Obviously," said Rosie, "someone was down here. Maybe they were tapping on the door at y*our* end of the tunnel."

Viola lit up. "Then that would mean this end isn't a wall. It's got to be another door."

"Leading where?" said Sylvester.

"Well, we know we're facing northeast," said Viola. "We figured that out a long time ago. The tunnel didn't bend, so wherever we are must be directly across the street and uphill from my house."

"No way!" said Sylvester. "Then that means—"

But Woodrow had already begun to push at the wooden wall. Slowly it began to open. A crack of light appeared at the side, and before they knew it, the group was staring into the basement of another house. "This is the Reynolds place!" said Viola.

The room was about the same size as Viola's basement. However, this basement was furnished.

Wood paneling lined the walls. Books were stacked in haphazard piles everywhere. A carpeted staircase rose up just a few feet away from where they stood, presumably to the house's main floor. It was strange how ordinary the place looked, considering the circumstances.

"You guys," said Woodrow, "if the sounds that Viola heard at night were someone tapping against the door of the tunnel in her basement, then that means someone must have been banging on something down here tonight. The sound probably echoed through the tunnel."

"Then they're here!" said Sylvester. "What if they *are* burglars? What if they catch us?"

The door at the top of the stairs creaked open, and the kids froze, collectively holding their breath. The highest step squeaked as, unseen, someone slowly stepped onto it. Whoever it was began to cautiously descend. None of the kids knew what to do. They were as curious as they were terrified.

Finally, two legs appeared on the stairs, followed by the hem of a long skirt. The unknown woman paused, as if listening, then continued down. Viola noticed she was holding something at her side. A hammer!

As quietly as possible, Viola pushed her friends back into the tunnel. Then, the woman shrieked—a piercing, glass-shattering cry. Viola turned to look, trying to pull the door shut behind them. She caught a glimpse of the woman, now at the bottom of the stairs. The woman had raised the hammer and was coming at them. Disheveled blond braids slipped down from a pile on top of her head. Her dark eyes were open wide. Viola screamed a bit herself, then they all turned and ran back down the dark tunnel, the flashlight swinging and swaying dizzily in Woodrow's grasp, creating jagged shadows that made the walls seem like they were falling down.

When they reached the entrance to Viola's basement, they heard a voice call to them from up the tunnel.

"Hello?" said the woman. The word bounced against the stones, becoming more and more ominous as it faded into the darkness. The group paused, shocked that someone who had been about to murder them all now seemed ready to greet them.

"We need to get out of here!" said Sylvester.

"Wait," said Viola, her heart racing, trying to catch her breath. "Let's just calm down for a minute."

"But Fiona's coming!" cried Rosie, inching toward the staircase.

"I think we let our nerves get the better of us," said Viola. "I know who this woman is. And it's not Fiona Hauptmann."

"If it's not her, then who is it?" asked Rosie.

Seconds later, a figure appeared in the doorway behind the wooden shelving unit. Viola had seen her face earlier that day on her way home from school. Betsy Ulrich—the Realtor who was selling the Reynolds house. Her picture was plastered on the For Sale sign across the street. Now, though, her hair was a mess, those extravagant braids having fallen apart in the chase.

After a moment, Viola noticed that the entire group recognized her. Still, they were in shock. They'd had quite a scare.

"I'm so sorry," said Betsy, still clutching the hammer. "But you frightened me. I'd gone upstairs to check on some paperwork, and I heard whispering in the basement. When I came back down the stairs, I saw you all disappear into that hole in the wall. I didn't know what to think."

"So you tried to kill us?" cried Sylvester.

"No!" said Betsy, appalled. "I would never! You scared me, and I reacted. Imagine going into your basement and finding me peeking out of a secret door at you! Victor told me about this old tunnel, but I didn't expect to find anyone using it. He'd explored it several times and assured me that the other end had been sealed off."

"Oh," Sylvester muttered. "Sorry."

"Then Victor was the one who was making

the noises all this time," Viola exclaimed. "He's my ghost!"

"Ghost?" Betsy looked confused and a little embarrassed. She shook her head. "I was just organizing for the open house we're having tomorrow." She held up the hammer. "Hanging pictures to give it some design appeal. The previous owner, Nelson, wasn't one for decorating. Obviously." She glanced around at the Harts' basement, as if suddenly understanding where she stood. "These old places have quirks, some of them dating back to the time of the Underground Railroad. I'm not sure if I should list this tunnel as a selling point for the Reynolds house. Some people might get freaked out."

"You think?" said Sylvester.

Woodrow nudged him, silently telling him to shut it.

"Which one of you lives here?" Betsy asked. Viola raised her hand. "No one told you this tunnel existed?"

"I don't think anyone knew. The previous owners thought the place was haunted. They heard noises. But I guess it was probably just Nelson poking around in his basement . . . or even inside the tunnel itself."

A few minutes later, Viola's parents came home to discover the small group standing in their basement. To say they were shocked that a secret passage had been hidden behind the built-in wooden shelves would have been an understatement, but they were also impressed that Viola and her friends had discovered it. Unfortunately for the group, they immediately determined that the tunnel was off-limits—at least until its safety could be confirmed.

Mr. and Mrs. Hart apologized to Betsy Ulrich for interrupting her work, and Betsy Ulrich apologized to the kids for frightening them. Just before the Realtor said good-bye, she handed Mr. Hart her business card. "In case you ever want to sell," she told him.

Viola was happy to hear his response.

"Oh, we don't plan on going anywhere anytime soon."

One Saturday a couple of weeks later, the trees were nearly bare. The familiar patch on the lawn where the four properties met was covered with colorful leaves. Each member of the Question Marks Mystery Club stood, armed with rakes. Their parents had asked them to come together for a common goal. Nothing mysterious this time—they were simply supposed to clean up the yards.

Viola, however, had ulterior motives. Before any of them had a chance to touch their rakes to the ground, she spoke up. "I have news," she said, with an enigmatic lilt in her voice.

Sylvester, Woodrow, and Rosie suddenly perked up. Whenever Viola said something like this, they knew it was going to be good.

"I didn't tell you guys, but after the incident with the black car in the garage across the street, my mom made me write a letter to Vincent Reynolds in New Hampshire to apologize for trespassing on his property. In my letter, I did mention I was sorry . . . but I also decided it would be the perfect opportunity to ask him some questions. He wrote back!

"He confirmed that he was the one who had been knocking around, explaining that he remembered his brother saying something about the house's secret passage. Vincent keeps strange hours, he says, because he has a hard time sleeping. He didn't realize that I could hear his nighttime explorations of the basement and the tunnel. And he thought the door at the other end had been sealed off a long time ago. But he kept coming back to it, wondering what was on the other side. I guess he had no idea that if only he'd pushed hard enough, he would have found out.

"His response got me thinking. What was the tunnel used for, anyway? The Realtor, Betsy Ulrich, told us that it dated back to the secret Underground Railroad, so the original owners must have helped smuggle runaway slaves into Canada.

"The wires and the light sockets that are in the tunnel now tell a different story, though. The tunnel must have been used by someone within the past century. For what? I thought about it for a long time and, as usual, I came up with a theory. After I wrote to Vincent one more time, he responded and told me that I was right."

"What was your theory?" Rosie asked, clutching the handle of her rake so hard that her knuckles had turned pale.

"Our mystery has one final clue. And it's right here in our yard."

"Here?" said Sylvester, glancing around. "Where?"

Viola continued as if she had planned this speech and would not be interrupted, which was, in fact, what she'd done. "I believe it explains everything we need to know about the secret of the tunnel in my basement. Can you guys guess what it is?"

Sylvester, Woodrow, and Rosie looked at one another with confused determination. Since the end of the summer, they had solved a dog-napping and discovered a forged autograph. They had revealed a faked photograph and dispensed with a couple of phony psychics. They had learned the true nature of a couple of haunting experiences. They must figure out Viola's latest clue—they were members of the Question Marks, after all.

"A clue to the mystery of the tunnel...," Woodrow whispered, dragging his rake behind him as he began to wander around the yard.

"What could it be?" said Rosie, swiveling swiftly on her heels, turning toward each compass direction, trying to decide which way to walk.

Sylvester stood still and closed his eyes, as if what he saw in his mind was more powerful than what was all around him.

Viola simply crossed her arms and smiled. She knew they'd figure it out eventually.

Can you?

Rosie suddenly spun, facing the street beside Viola and Sylvester's house, along the northwest quadrant of their yards. "You guys!" she called. Woodrow and Sylvester rushed over to her. She whispered in their ears, then they all whipped their heads toward the maple tree near the road—the one where they had come together for the very first time on the day Viola moved to Moon Hollow.

Slowly, the three of them walked to the tree. Viola followed not far behind, unable to make out what they were saying to one another. Finally, standing at the base of the maple, they all met again.

"So?" asked Viola. "What do you think?"

Rosie pointed up, at where someone had long ago carved initials into the bark.

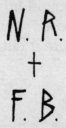

"And?" said Viola, smiling.

"They're Nelson Reynolds and Fiona Hauptmann!" said Sylvester.

"Actually," Woodrow said, patting the tree trunk, "it would have been Nelson Reynolds and Fiona Branson, right, Viola? That's what you said her name was originally, before she got married."

"Uh-huh. So what does that mean?" Viola asked, teasing them.

"It means that when they were young," said Rosie, "they were in love." The boys gave her a funny look. "Or something. They carved their initials into the tree trunk to prove it to each other."

"Yeah," Sylvester added. "But they didn't end up together. Fiona got married to someone else."

"Right," said Woodrow. "To Mr. Hauptmann, who died a long time ago. She ended up alone. Or so everybody thought."

"And the tunnel?" Viola said.

The group thought for a few seconds. Then Rosie spoke up. "Obviously, they both knew about it. They lived most of their lives in these two houses." She pointed up the hill. "Maybe they *weren't* alone. We know that Nelson was secretive and kept to himself. What if, when they grew older, they fell in love again? Maybe they used the passage to travel between their homes."

Woodrow added, "That's why the tunnel was wired with light sockets!"

"Then," Sylvester said, excited, "when Fiona passed away, new people moved into her house. They must not have known the secret passage existed. At night, they could hear Nelson moving around through the tunnel. Maybe he thought if he looked hard enough for her, he'd find her again. That's got to be why people claimed Viola's house was haunted. Both of the Reynolds brothers have been freaking out the new owners for the past few years!"

Viola was silent for a few seconds, admiring her new friends. Then she spoke. "That's what Vincent told me. Or at least the part about Fiona and Nelson being together once they got older. They acted like a married couple — they actually shared the houses. I doubt Vincent knew much more than that, since his brother was such a mystery to everyone. But you guys were right. This tree was the final clue to the haunting of the Hart house."

Just then, Rosie's father called to her from his back patio. "Hey! The lawn's not going to rake itself!"

Rosie was mortified. "He was kidding. . . . I think."

"Maybe we should get to work," said Viola. "My mom did promise us pizza if we fill ten bags."

"Only ten?" Sylvester scoffed. "I can fill twenty!" The others glanced at one another, raising their eyebrows.

"You go right ahead," said Woodrow. "We'll keep count."

"Har-har-har," Sylvester answered, dragging his rake across the roots of the tree. "Did I mention I can also eat a whole pizza? There might be none left for you."

"That's what you think!" Woodrow raised his rake and said, "En garde!" The two boys began to spar.

"Boys!" whispered Rosie to Viola, rolling her eyes and leading the way back to the place where the four yards met. That's where they started clearing away the leaves, pulling hard against the stubborn grass.

The kids worked all afternoon, until the day grew dark, filling bag after bag with fallen leaves. Finally, they had only enough leaves to form one last pile. Rosie held a bag open, and Sylvester was about to scoop the pile inside when a gust of wind raced through the yard, scattering their work across the grass. Woodrow chased after the mess with his rake, as if he could stop what had already happened. The wind carried most of the leaves out to the street, where they scuttled and eddied toward town, swirling and dancing past houses and shops, street signs and parked cars, across the train tracks that led south to the big city, then farther, out to the river.

Viola and her friends watched as the street-lights blinked on all around them, illuminating the shadows of Moon Hollow. Still, most of the buildings down the street remained dark. Viola wondered how many secrets were hidden inside them. If the number was even half as large as she imagined, she knew the Question Marks would be busy all autumn long.

ABOUT THE AUTHOR

Dan Poblocki is the author of *The Stone Child* and *The Nightmarys*. Like many writers, he's had a long list of strange jobs. Dan has traveled New Jersey as a bathing suit salesman, played the role of Ichabod Crane in a national tour of *The Legend of Sleepy Hollow*, wrangled the audience for *Who Wants to Be a Millionaire?*, sold snacks at *The Lion King*'s theater on Broadway, recommended books at Barnes & Noble, answered phones for Columbia University, and done research at Memorial Sloan-Kettering Cancer Center. He has never been a detective though, and after writing this book, he thinks he might just give it a try.

Visit the author at www.danpoblocki.com.

The mysteries don't end here!
Viola, Rosie, Sylvester, and Woodrow are in for
even greater challenges when they uncover a
surprising secret—one that has them looking at
their neighbors in a whole new light.
Who can they really trust?
Find out in . . .

The MYSTERIOUS FOUR

CLOCKS and ROBBERS

Available July 2011

1

THE STRANGERS GAME

A spherical clock has sat atop a tall black iron pedestal in front of the Moon Hollow Public Library for as long as anyone can remember. The clock's large, ornately designed, four-sided face gazes unassumingly upon busy and bustling Maple Street, where shops, restaurants, and office buildings stand side by side like books shoved tightly onto a shelf.

One day in early November, a girl named Rosie Smithers watched from the sidewalk as the four big clock hands leapt ahead five minutes in less than five seconds. Four loud chimes rang out and echoed up the street with stern authority.

Like the clock's pedestal, Rosie was also tall and thin. Her skin was the color of cocoa. Her hair was long and twisted into braids that fell to her shoulders. "Did you see that?" she asked, turning to her friend Viola Hart. They had been waiting for Mrs. Smithers, the town librarian, to get out of work.

"See what?" Viola answered. Her eyes grew wide with excitement. Viola was a smallish girl with a burst of red curls on top of her head and freckles on her pale cheeks.

"The minute hand on that big clock was stuck at three fifty-five for a while," Rosie explained. "Then, it jumped forward to four o'clock."

"The minute hand *jumped*?" Viola asked. From her knapsack, she pulled out a black-and-white composition notebook and pen. Flipping the book open, she carefully jotted down a note.

Rosie recited what had recently become Viola's motto: "Mysteries are everywhere if you look for them."

Surprised, Viola laughed. "I was just about to say that!"

"I know." Rosie smiled. "I see that notebook, and I know what's coming."

"I'm no mystery, I guess." Viola shrugged. "But what about the clock?"

"You think?" Rosie squinted as she glanced across the street. "That *would* be a fun mystery. It's probably just broken though."

Viola raised an eyebrow. As they'd recently learned, anything might be a clue to a great big secret. In fact, that was the reason the girls were waiting for Mrs. Smithers across the street from the library.

During lunch that day, Viola had come up with a new contest she'd named the Strangers Game. The point was to observe people they didn't know, and try to guess who they were. So far, the girls had secretly watched a disheveled young woman carrying a huge load of picture books as she exited the library. She didn't look old enough to have kids of her own, and she definitely was not a teacher at their school. So who would the woman share picture books with, other than some kids she was watching? They guessed she must be a babysitter—probably a student at the college who needed some extra cash.

"I've got another one," Viola proclaimed, nodding at the library's entrance. "I see a woman who has a huge family, works really hard, loves cooking, and records soap operas during the day so she can watch them later at night."

All those details sounded vaguely familiar to Rosie . . . and very specific. "How did you figure all that out?" she asked, glancing up and down the street for someone who might fit the description.

Viola giggled as the woman who was standing in the library's entrance waved at them. "She's my next door neighbor."

"Hey!" said Rosie, noticing her mother heading toward them across the plaza and past the broken clock. "My mom? That's cheating!"

"Well . . . just a little." Viola winked.

When he'd gotten to his parents' diner after school, Sylvester Cho had found an odd-looking man sitting alone at a booth, drinking a cup of coffee. The man wore a black T-shirt and had a scruffy beard. His arms were covered with colorful tattoos. Sylvester immediately deduced that the man was in a biker gang. He kept watch on him, in case the man made trouble. But a few minutes later, a beautiful young woman in a flowing green dress, a black velvet jacket, and a thick gray scarf entered the diner. She was pushing a stroller. The man had stood up, kissed the woman, and then lifted a tiny baby from the carriage. "Did you miss your daddy?" he asked the infant, then cooed.

Instantly, Sylvester realized that he'd been wrong about the man. Tattoos and a beard didn't mean he was a bad guy . . . or even that he rode a motorcycle. In fact, a few minutes later, when the family stood to go, Sylvester noticed the man grab a satchel from under the table. A logo on it read: *Hudson Valley Country Day School.* Paintbrushes, pencils, and rolled-up paper poked out from the bag's canvas flap. The man was obviously an artist, and probably a teacher!

Sylvester couldn't wait to tell his friends what he'd learned: Sometimes people are not what they seem.

The phone rang, bringing Sylvester back to reality. Mr. Cho answered it. "Hi, Honey." It was Sylvester's mother, who had taken his baby sister, Gwen, to visit his grandmother, Hal-muh-ni, just outside of New York City. Listening in on his parents' conversation, Sylvester started to rearrange plates on a nearby table. Behind the long counter, his father turned his back and edged away from Sylvester, tensing up. Sylvester paid even closer attention as his father lowered his voice, saying, "She agreed? Well that's great news, isn't it?" Mr. Cho glanced at Sylvester, who quickly looked back at the table he was pretending to clean. "No," he continued, in an even lower voice. "I haven't mentioned it to him yet."

Now Sylvester was even more curious.

Mr. Cho hung up the phone and turned back to Sylvester. "I assume you heard all that?" his father asked. Sylvester nodded. "So what do you think?" his father asked.

"About?" Sylvester said. Should he have known what his father meant? Had he missed a clue?

"About your grandmother coming to live with us?"

"Hal-muh-ni?" said Sylvester, immediately thinking how cool that would be. Then another thought popped into his head. "But where will she stay?" Their house had three bedrooms, and each one was currently taken.

Mr. Cho was silent for a few seconds. "We were thinking she would stay in your room."

"My room?" Sylvester said.

"We can fix up the basement for you instead. Your own private spot. Sound good?"

"You want me to move into . . . the *basement*?" From behind the counter, Sylvester's father stared back at him with an uncomfortable smile. How long had his parents been planning this? How long had they kept this secret? And how could they do this to him . . . shove him away in a dark corner of the house, like an unfortunate character in a creepy fantasy story by Roald Dahl or Lemony Snicket or Neil Gaiman? Sure, having his own private spot might be interesting, but after what the Question Marks had been through in the past couple of months, he knew how disturbing a basement could be. Sylvester reached out and straightened some silverware on a nearby table. He suddenly realized he'd been right: Sometimes people are not what they seem, even people you've known all your life.

That morning, Mrs. Knox had asked Woodrow to come home after school and start cleaning up the house. Woodrow had a habit of leaving his stuff in random places—comic books in the living room, video games in the den, schoolwork on the kitchen table, sports equipment on the floor. His mom had said she would have a surprise for him that evening, and as Woodrow worked, he wondered what it might be. He was hoping for a flat-screen television.

Woodrow was nearly finished tucking his little messes out of sight when he heard the car pull into the driveway. He rushed to the front door. Swinging it open, Woodrow noticed not one car parked in front of the garage, but two. Behind his mother's forest green SUV was a bright red Mini Cooper. A man got out of it and rushed to open Mrs. Knox's door. The man was tall. He wore a tweed jacket and dark blue jeans. His sandy blond hair was close-cropped and combed tightly to the side. Mrs. Knox hopped out of her own car, then nodded toward Woodrow, who stood on the front porch. The tall man turned, smiled at him, and waved.

Woodrow blinked, contemplating what this might mean. Viola's new contest, the Strangers Game, popped into his head. *Notice the details of this man. Figure out who he is.* Obviously, the man was *not* here to deliver a flat-screen television . . . or anything else, for that matter. His car was barely big enough to fit another person inside it; he probably didn't have any kids. He was dressed well—too well, as if he wanted to impress someone. As they came up the front walkway toward Woodrow, the man lightly touched his mom's elbow. They were smiling in an unnatural way—too many teeth. Woodrow had seen his mom wear the same expression the day she had interviewed for her current job. He realized what those smiles meant: These people were terrified.

Slowly, the clues began to click into place. He could deal with the surprise not being what he'd hoped. Easy. You can't mourn a television that never belonged to you. But he wasn't sure if he was ready to meet his mom's new boyfriend. And all the signs indicated that this stranger on the front walk was his mom's big surprise.

"Woodrow," said his mom, leading the tall man up the stairs, "I want you to meet my friend Bill. We're all going to have dinner here tonight. Together."

From the porch stairs, Bill extended his hand. "Nice to meet you, Woodrow. Your mom's a pretty cool lady." Mrs. Knox laughed, a little too loudly.

"I know that," said Woodrow, shaking Bill's hand like his father had taught him. He squeezed hard. "Nice to meet you too."

Woodrow wasn't sure if he liked Viola's new game. Maybe sometimes strangers should remain strangers.

Even so, he wanted to tell Sylvester, Rosie, and Viola about this. He knew it was only a matter of time before they all met again.

As it turned out, the next morning, Woodrow got his wish.